Written in the Stars

Brenna

Lyons

Star Mages #1

Fireborn Publishing Copyright Statement

peer or other pirate sites, even those masquerading as legitimate retailers, please let us know at sales@firebornpublishing.com or via the author's personal email.

All characters and events in this book are fictitious. Any resemblance to actual persons, living or dead, is strictly coincidental.

This book is written in US English.

PUBLISHER

Dedicated to...

Lisa, who indulged in years of musicals with me and first introduced me to Victor/Victoria.

LaMont Arnold, who scheduled a musical every spring for our theatre group and cultivated my love of the style.

My SCAdian friends, who taught me to filk. I've never looked back.

Notes About the Series

Names are pronounced how they appear, with one notable exception. Caiben is pronounced Kie-ben (much like a gentleman I know named Kai is pronounced Kie).

The levels of Star Mages and their color marks are as follows:

Trainee Mage- White

Apprentice Mage- Purple

Midman Mage- Green—You cannot advance past Midman without sealing; the lowest rank at which you can wander without a Master Mage or join the King's service.

Mason Mage- Brown

Master Mage- Black—Can only be reached after a test of power with the king and his blessing of robes.

Great Mage- Red—Can only be reached when the strongest Mages of a Great house duel for leadership. Male children of a Great house are always given a name beginning with the house name in anticipation of leadership of the house.

Royal house- Star Blue, a color not unlike baby blue

Every month on Terra Set consists of an even thirty-two days, four eight-day weeks. Days on Terra Set consist of one-third daylight and two-thirds night. This is largely due to the close-set planets and moons in the solar system, blocking sunlight that might have reached the planet's surface.

Prologue

Ellien's Ease

In Written in The Stars, I talk about how Riena is con- ceived, in general terms, but the image of the widow and widower taking solace in each other has always haunted me. It's time that Ellien was given a voice.

Ellien paused, the platter of hot food balanced on her arm.

The Great Mage Andren sat cross-legged in the field, his red robes opened to his waist, staring at the moon with a near-heartbreaking look on his beautiful face. He was of the typical slight build, his face and chest smooth and hairless. Like all Mages, he had dark eyes, pale skin, and dark hair that hung loose around his shoulders. Andren's was heavily streaked with gray, though she couldn't guess if it was due to his age—impossible to surmise, given his appearance as a Mage—or the great strain he found himself under.

"What do you want, woman?" his companion barked.

She jumped, nearly overturning the tray in surprise. He moved quietly for so massive a man, as quietly as she imagined Andren's usual royal bodyguard would move.

He advanced, forcing her back another step. "I asked you a question, farmer's daughter."

"F-food," she stammered. "My father bid me bring Great Mage Andren his meal, as was agreed.

1

You can collect the rest on the morrow...at your leisure."

"And, does your father bid you bring other comforts, as well?" He scowled, making his meaning and his disapproval clear in a single look.

Her face heated. "Nay! My father would never—"

"Would he not?" he taunted.

Even had she been willing to consider such a thing, her father would never have suggested it to her. Telan doted on her and always had; he would never have suggested something that would cause her unease.

"Does a father often push widows in mourning sashes at an unwilling mourning Mage?" she countered hotly.

A knot rose in her throat at the thought of Regald, and she blinked back tears. She would not give this oaf the satisfaction of seeing how the very thought of what he accused could wound her. To him, she was a farmer's daughter, a scheming vixen in search of a Mage's seed.

"Let her through, Elden."

Ellien snapped her gaze to the Great Mage, then bowed her head reverently.

"Bring the tray," he continued.

The companion backed off a pace, and Ellien rounded him, lowering the tray to the ground within Andren's reach. She started to rise.

"Stay a while," he requested, waving his companion away.

"I would not presume to impose myself upon your grief," Ellien whispered in response.

"I should..." He sighed. "I should like to speak with another who suffers."

She nodded, settling to the ground. "If it pleases you."

Andren shook his head, his jaw tightening. "I fear nothing pleases me now."

"Were you... Apologies, Great One. It was an impertinent question and one I have no right to pose."

"Soulbound?" He looked back to the moon. "Yes. We were."

Ellien considered her response carefully. Offering her sympathies that he'd soulbound would offend him. A Star Mage's happiest memories were those of his soulbound years and the act of meeting the Grand Rebirth of Mother Moon to bind. Yet losing the other half of your soul was excruciating, something unable to be borne for long. "I understand," she whispered.

He stared at her, his expression unreadable.

"I do not," she conceded. "How could I?" Losing Regald didn't mean she'd follow him to death, though she'd mused it might be easier than the pain of his loss more than once in the last ten moon cycles.

A touch of a smile softened his face. "Then you are wiser than most, with their empty words and false smiles."

"That is nearly the worst of it," she agreed. It almost seemed a happier thing for Andren to travel, isolated this way, than to face the likes of it.

"Yes. It is."

3

There was a moment of silence between them, though not an uncomfortable one. Andren took a slice of roast from the tray and chewed on it.

The movement uncovered more of his chest to the strength of the moon's radiance at a simple night of rebirth. Ellien wondered at that. She'd met lesser Star Mages before. Unless they were channeling their magic into the plants and soil, they typically covered most of their skin to a strong moon such as this. The alternative, she'd been told, was very uncomfortable.

Andren met her eyes, and she looked away. It wouldn't do to appear rude.

"What is your name?" he asked.

"Ellien."

"Of?" he prodded after a moment of awaiting more.

"Bentin. My husband was Regald of Bentin."

"The Bentin are fine farmers," he noted simply.

"Yes. He was." Regald had also been a doting husband and a fine father, but Ellien didn't want to hear reminders of it from someone who couldn't know it...or even someone who could. She'd heard too much of it, empty words, meaningless platitudes.

Another silence fell, and Andren partook of fruit and ale. "Suson was my mate." He said it simply, without embellishment or show of emotion.

Ellien nodded, at a loss to comment. She had no clue what family the woman might have hailed from. Even had she, the affairs of noble families had never been of interest to her. And it was unlikely that Andren wanted to hear compliments. If she didn't, it only stood to reason that he would feel similarly about the subject.

"She has been gone more than a season."

"So long?" Ellien managed in shock. How could he survive so long with his soul ripped in two?

Andren nodded, setting down his cup of ale. "And yours?" His inquiry was polite, but she sensed that he sought something in it.

"Ten moon cycles and four nights."

He panned his gaze from her face to the white sash of mourning at her waist. "Yet, your father has not shaken you from grief? He is a rare man to allow you so long in your pain."

Ellien managed a strained smile. "I think he means to keep me close in his waning years, and I *know* he sees my son as an asset he would have for his land and not another's."

"You have a son."

"Rosher," she supplied. "He is eleven years."

"Have you any others?"

"No. The Mother never blessed us again." She studied his wistful smile. "And you?" she asked bluntly. "Did The Mother bless you and your Suson?"

"Repeatedly. I have two sons and two daughters. All are grown or nearly so."

What could she say to that? It was wonderful and yet tragic. The only blessing was that he'd seen them grow. The need to laugh warred with the tears stinging her eyes, and her face felt pulled into one expression after another.

"You do understand." His voice held a note of relief. "I have long prayed for someone who would."

Ellien swallowed a lump in her throat. "If it gives you ease, I thank The Mother that I can."

"Even though it is *your* pain that allows it?"

"Is it better to feel pain alone or shared? Your prayers indicate that you agree shared is better."

"You are very wise, Ellien of Bentin."

"If I am, I have simply learned life's lessons well."

"Thus grows most wisdom."

"Yes. Most probably. Such a pity that it seems the only way." She looked to the moon, marveling at the beauty and power of The Mother.

"What are you thinking, Ellien?"

She met his eyes, her gaze trailing to his bare chest from there. "How is it that you can soak up Mother Moon's radiance this way, when She is so strong? Is it because you are a Great Mage?" Ellien blushed, abruptly aware that she sounded like a curious child or the uneducated farmer's daughter she undeniably was.

He chuckled. "Even I am not that strong. Even Evard is not."

She winced at the near-sacrilege of saying such a thing about the king but held her tongue. No doubt, Andren knew King Evard well; they were cousins of a sort, after all.

"I am channeling the magic slowly into your father's lands."

"But, why... This—this is a tremendous strain, and..."

"And? The strain is not so much. It gives me purpose for the time The Mother grants me here. Why should I not do it?"

"There was no payment," she protested.

"I have no need of money."

"Yes. I suppose that is true. You did request much less for your service than even a Mason Mage would have." Considering the fact that he was on a mourning pilgrimage, that wasn't surprising. "But, it is too much gift to—"

"Consider your company as equal trade. It means more to me than the outlay of power."

Ellien looked to the moon again, her emotions rioting at the thought that anyone would think a bit of conversation as precious as what several bags of gold would not typically buy. "Then I thank you. This will mean a lot to my father and brother."

"What would mean a lot to you, Ellien?"

She sighed. "Nothing you can give, I fear, just as nothing I can give would bring you true joy."

"There are always memories," he continued, heedless of her dismissal. "There are always shades of what once made us happy."

Ellien considered that. "Some nights, happy memories are all that make life worth another day."

Andren moved to her side. "Indeed, they do. Tell me your most precious memory, Ellien. I have coin enough to make it again."

Her cheeks darkened. "It is not a matter that gold can make, though I thank you for your concern."

7

He turned her face toward him; her skin tingled in the glow of his magic.

"Tell me," he requested.

It sounded as if his very existence into the moonset depended on an answer, and so she gave him one. "Regald set aside a portion of his land for me. He... It was ridiculous, something no farmer would do. His father was livid."

"Tell me." His eyes pleaded with her to continue.

"He planted a bed of flowers for me, seasonals so there would always be color and sweet smells for me, even if I had to brush away the early snows to find them."

Andren smiled. "That is all?"

Her cheeks burned fiercely in the memory of how Regald used those flowers to bring her pleasure.

"I see," he whispered.

Ellien didn't doubt that he did. *And he no doubt also sees why he can never make the memory for me again.* Her heart ached in the loss of the promise, though she'd always known it was impossible.

The scent of flowers teased her first. Soft petals appeared around her without sprouting and growing first. The numb realization that he was transforming the winter crops around them to a field of flowers shook her when it settled fully in her mind.

Andren was incredibly powerful. Few Mages could transform the essence of one plant to that of another, let alone countless others as a field of flowers demanded of him.

8

They thickened, strengthened, their scent intensifying. The net of their roots spread, and new blooms appeared between the rows, creating a solid mat of silken blooms. Ellien gasped as they shifted her, lifting her from the dirt, the work of a hundred hands and more making light the task. And still, they grew.

Andren's eyes reflected a hunger, a want that Ellien thought she'd never see in a man's eyes again. Without a thought, she touched his chest, pushing his robes from his shoulders.

His mouth covered hers, the kiss of a man who needs desperately. She didn't deny him. How could she, when they could offer each other such comfort?

It is a fleeting thing, the joining of bodies for but a night. Ellien didn't delude herself that it could be more than that. Andren had been soulbound to Suson. His heart and soul belonged to another, but his body and battered mind demanded what ease she could provide.

There were no questions between them, no rationalization of what they were doing. Andren untied her mourning sash and pushed up at her dress, following her down onto the thick quilt of fragrant flowers.

Her dress retreated further, and his body pressed to hers, smooth skin brushing her flesh. His hands left her for a moment, then returned, waking her to the pleasures she'd all but forgotten existed between a man and woman.

The head of his cock pressed to her seam, and she rose to meet him.

"Andren, please," she begged.

He was inside her in one fierce thrust. She cried out at the sensation of his magic massaging her inner muscles, sensitizing her to his touch. It was a wonderful gift, and she wanted more. Ellien wrapped her arms and legs around him, urging him on toward climax, meeting his thrusts. He groaned as climax took her, following moments later. His heat buffeted the magic-soaked walls of her sheath, making her weak in continuing waves of release. Sparks of his magic surrounded her and filled her.

It was unlike anything she'd experienced with Regald. That fact alone expunged the slight sense of guilt at taking Andren in his place in such a way.

In the aftermath, the flowers' scent seemed to intensify, a heady fragrance that made her head swim.

Andren traced the line of her lower lip with his sensitive fingertips. "You give me such ease," he whispered.

"I regret only that it cannot last," she countered. "Just as these flowers cannot."

His brow furrowed. "Why should they not?"

"My father is a practical man, a rational man with an eye to his accounts. He will reclaim this ground, just as Regald's father reclaimed that which my husband planted and tended for me." That simply, her sadness returned.

A look of determination settled on his fine features. "He will *never* reclaim this land."

"Andren?" She winced, then reasoned that they'd known such intimacy as to make familiar address expected.

Still, what could he be thinking? Telan of Gerin would never sell this land to the Great Mage as a gift to her, at any price, not even to see Ellien happy.

"Give me ease once more, Ellien. Give me ease, and I will weave a magic your father will never break. Not with a hundred rebirths and a thousand Star Mages will he undo it."

The concept stunned her to silence.

"Will you give me ease once more?"

She nodded shakily. "I will, Andren. I will give you ease." *And ease us both in the bargain.*

* * * *

Ellien looked at the setting moon, laughing aloud, tears misting her eyes. The scent of her flowers washed over her, even from a distance, and she said a silent thanks to Andren yet again. She added one to The Mother hurriedly, not wanting to insult the kind benefactress so.

True to Andren's vow, the magic could not be undone. The flowers endured all, rising renewed at every moonrise, despite her father's attempts to reclaim the land. In the end, after more than a moon cycle of trying to destroy them, Telan had grudgingly conceded that the increased production of the other fields more than made up for the loss of the one.

She picked up her mourning sash, biting back a new peel of mirth. How could she wear such a thing, when all was so very right in her world? When there was such joy in her heart?

Determined, she marched to the kitchen with it in her hand. It was time for a change. "Long past time."

Belin didn't look up when she entered the room. Her younger brother by three years was busy building up the fire as she would have done more than an hour earlier on any normal morning. This was not a normal morning. Even their father must have felt something of the difference and as such had ordered Belin not to wake her to her chores.

"You slept late," Belin noted, his voice cold and clipped.

"I did." She answered in kind.

"I sent Rosher to his chores."

"My thanks for it." He'd no doubt done it without allowing her son food in punishment, but she would right that soon enough.

Telan looked up from his accounts, assessing her. "Are you well, Ellien? You look pale, and it is unlike you to miss the start of day."

"Quite well, Father." She was. Despite her discomfort, she felt she could fly to Mother Moon.

Ellien didn't hesitate. She reached around Belin's shoulder and threw her mourning sash into the red-orange flames of the new fire, watching them lick up its length and burn white-hot for a long moment.

Belin turned abruptly, his look calculating. She could nearly follow his thoughts through the expense of hiring a woman to do her work if she left them again, weighed against the loathsome-to-him option of marrying and bringing a wife home to do what they would otherwise have to hire out for.

Her father's voice broke the moment between them...and added to the tension in the room at the same time. "You have decided to take another husband?" he inquired.

"I have not. I believe I will never do that," she assured him, smiling in her unbridled joy.

"Then what?" He watched her warily.

Ellien's smile spread in spite of the near threat of violence in the air around her. "I carry a child."

Belin muttered a series of curses.

Telan took to his feet, his jaw tight in fury. "What man fathered it?"

"You need not fear a claim on your land, Father. Great Mage Andren is the sire."

His anger melted into shock, then to a look of calculation that rivaled Belin's. His thoughts were no harder to gauge. The prospect of a young Star Mage, in service to Telan and his lands until the age of adulthood, was quite the prize, especially when it was the child of one as powerful as Andren. Such a thing was beyond comprehension, impossible to lay a price to. And the fact that she meant not to marry again indicated that the child would be Telan's to order.

Her father's expression settled on one she'd seen often, the pride he'd always had for her. "Well met, Ellien."

She darkened at the inference that she'd planned this, as Andren's companion had once accused she would, as many farmer's daughters conspired to win heirs of Star Mages. Ellien straightened, raising her chin in challenge. "Believe what you will of me."

Telan crossed the room, taking Ellien's hands in his own and guiding her to the table. "Belin, fetch milk and bread. No doubt, your sister's pallor may be attributed to the complaints of the Great Mage's son."

Belin grumbled complaints, but he complied, plunking the mug of milk down before her so that it sloshed over onto her sleeve. She didn't need to hear his words to guess that her brother envisioned himself a slave sold into the service of a young Mage already.

"Now," Telan continued. "All due care will be taken with this child, of course."

"Of course," Belin mimicked. "I suppose the boy and I will be drawing water and lifting—"

"Enough!"

Ellien jumped, her heart pounding. Their father rarely raised his voice. In truth, he rarely had to; no one tested him needlessly.

Telan handed Ellien a slab of bread left from the evening meal, patting her hand to calm her. "The flowers?" he hinted.

She cleared her throat, looking away from Belin's scowl. "A gift to me. Our child was conceived amidst them."

He chuckled, then laughed outright, long and hard. "I see. You must choose a proper name for one of House An...for the Great Mage's son...Andle or Angen."

"Anden." Ellien pressed a hand to her womb. She'd thought hard on the matter in the half moon cycle she'd waited for positive signs that her body was not simply off cycle. "Or Riena, for a girl." She'd always loved the name; she had intended to name her daughter Riena, had The Mother blessed her and Regald with one.

Belin snorted rudely. "You would produce a female, just to spite me," he accused.

Telan sighed. "If The Mother chooses to bless Ellien with a female, it is Her wish to do so. She will still be the daughter of a Great Mage and more likely to produce young Mages when she takes a husband or lover."

Ellien let them plot. It mattered not what they thought about her child. Andren had given her the greatest gift imaginable—not her flowers but hope and purpose as she hadn't felt since Regald's passing. He'd given her ease that would last past the moment, though she was incapable of doing the same for him.

Chapter One

Juno 16th, 4005

Riena skipped through the crops under the disappearing crescent of the moon, finding the flower circle where she'd been born effortlessly, even in the dim light of almost total night. She wasn't allowed to come here. Her grandfather would be furious that she had, but Riena didn't believe in silly superstitions, and tonight would be a Grand Rebirth of Mother Moon. When she'd been five, Riena hadn't understood why a Grand Rebirth was so significant to her. Now she was ten, and she knew the truth of who she was.

She'd heard some of the women in the village talking, hidden herself behind a basket of early fruits to hear it all. They didn't believe her grandfather's warnings that the circle was a sign of evil any more than Riena did. The women whispered about the magic of the circle, love magic.

The women from the village came to the circle quarterly, on the nights of rebirth, seeking the mother's blessing of a child with men they convinced to the flower circle with them. Her grandfather had chased many amorous couples from the circle, but tonight he would not venture near. On the night of the Grand Rebirth, not even her grandfather dared pass the borders of Ellien's ring of flowers.

The circle had been a near-barren spot far on the outreaches of her grandfather's land three seasons before Riena's birth. Then Great Mage

Andren passed through on his pilgrimage. On the night of the moon's rebirth, Andren brought strength to the land in exchange for three days at her grandfather's table and a week's worth of food upon leaving, much less than a Mage of his station would normally charge for such a service. Unknown to Grandfather at the time, Andren also enjoyed the comforts of Ellien's body and created a lush flower garden of their passion in that once-barren place.

When Ellien's time came, she took it as a sign that the moon would rebirth grand and went to her flowers to deliver Riena alone. The women whispered that Riena had been born in the Silver Minute, though surely no one could know that for certain.

They said her grandfather made a pyre of the circle to take her mother's cold body, but the flowers wouldn't burn. He tried cutting the flowers, poisoning them, and even plowing them under, but Ellien's flowers always appeared untouched at next moonrise.

Riena sobered at what else the women said. They said her grandfather would have thrown Riena to the pyre were it not for Rosher's pleas and Grandfather's fear of the Great Mage's magic protecting what was his. Her grandfather had sent for the Mage, anxious to be rid of Riena, but Andren's eldest son, the new Great Mage Andrel of house An, responded that his father was dead and refused responsibility for "a bastard that Andren likely hadn't sired."

Legally, Riena was her grandfather's responsibility, but more than that, he feared the magic that might protect her and had no wish to test its strength.

Riena's life had been comfortable but empty. She wasn't beaten or deprived of food and clothing, but the only love she knew was Rosher's. Ellien's son with her first mate acted as both mother and father to Riena, despite being only eleven years her senior.

Her grandfather and uncle preferred to ignore Riena's presence unless pressed by Rosher for money necessary to her upkeep. The villagers watched her warily, though Riena had no idea why they mistrusted her. Even the women hadn't divulged that.

She stilled in her wandering through the flowers, looking to the moon with a smile. Mother Moon was fully dark, an occurrence that never lasted long on Terra Set, where the nights were twice again as long as the days year-round and the light of the night sky almost as nourishing as the watery sunlight for supporting the food they ate—moreso if one considered the power of the Star Mages. Soon, the moon would rebirth as she did every three months, and the Silver Minute that only occurred at high summer every five years would be upon the world.

Riena lay back in the thick grass, careful not to crush too many of the flowers, in case the stories of their restorative powers were false. The first sliver of the moon reappeared, and Riena shouted her wish to the black sky that matched her Mage's hair. "Mother Moon! Grant me knowledge of my parents. I would know myself better by it." She laughed in joy as silver light raced over the countryside, brighter than the gray daylight of high summer, a season's worth of energy for the struggling crops in a few precious moments.

The wave reached her, and Riena's breath caught in surprise. The light was warm, and it seemed to trace her skin like a thousand fingertips. This was the power the Mages felt. She was certain that it was, but why could she feel it? Was this what she would know of her father? If so, it was precious.

"Riena." Rosher's voice was pleading but edged in annoyance. "If you do not return to your bed, Grandfather will assign you extra duties in punishment."

She didn't answer—couldn't answer in her state of rapture at the sensations of the Silver Minute.

"Riena," he warned, probably believing her hiding from him.

The warmth became a burning, the comfort of fingers akin to the touch of a cauter brand. Riena shook her head, unable to break her connection with the growing moon. Panic set in.

"Riena, answer me."

She would have given anything to answer Rosher. Riena opened her mouth to answer him, but her lungs refused to work. The pain intensified until she felt she'd incinerate. Surely, Mother Moon didn't mean for her to feel Ellien's pyre.

Feel it she did. Riena bowed up, venting a scream of pain and terror mixed, forcing the sound past lips that trembled and a throat that felt like iron in the blast of the forge. The fire blazed bright around her, searing her eyes with its heat.

The Silver Minute passed. She collapsed to the grass, gasping for breath as the fire sped away from her skin, lighting the fields, then disappearing into the black depths of the night. Riena wept. She should have known better than to ask the Goddess for such a frivolous wish.

"By the Mother," Rosher exclaimed. He was suddenly with her, smoothing Riena's hair and wiping tears from cheeks that felt raw. "Riena, speak to me. Are you well?"

Riena met his eyes, shivering in the sudden chill surrounding her. "I burned," she gasped.

He nodded, scooping Riena to his chest. "All will be well," he vowed.

All of her senses were overly sensitized. The moonlight seemed too bright. Rosher's touch was painful. The smell of flowers pressed in on her. Even the sound of her grandfather's shouting seemed too loud. Then sleep claimed her.

Rosher winced at his grandfather's look of fury. He'd known Riena's show of power would bring the old man's displeasure. He only hoped he could convince Telan not to punish Riena for what she was.

"Leave," Telan demanded. "Take that demon with you and leave."

"Grandfather," he reasoned.

"She's ruined us," he thundered. "Look at what she's done."

Rosher scanned his gaze over the fields of flowers, fields that had been bursting with grain until the Silver Minute claimed Riena as its own. The fields would have to be up-rooted and re-soiled before crops were planted again. Their food and earnings for the year were largely forfeit. Only the orchards, animals, and the coin they'd amassed over years of successful farming stood to supplement the dried food stores until next year.

He nodded. "But Riena is a Star Mage, Grandfather. The Master Mage in Verin can teach her. Until her twentieth year, you can trade Riena's services for whatever you wish, and our own crops will know no equal but the king's own in all of Voria. Is that not beyond price for a single year of lean times?"

"Trade what? Who wants fields of worthless flowers?" Telan scowled at Riena, as if she had a choice in what mayhem she loosed when tested this way.

"She is untrained. No young Mage is perfect."

Telan met Rosher's gaze. "Hear me well. I have tolerated this demon thus far only for the fine work you have offered for her keep, but I can ignore this foul omen no longer. I want you off of my land while Belin and I try to salvage what we can."

Rosher looked to his uncle in distaste. Telan hated Riena for taking away his precious Ellien, but this move wasn't Telan's alone. The old man feared Great Mage Andren's spirit watching over his child from the stars too much to do this without Belin's urging.

"Should I take her to the Master Mage and return with Riena in the spring to right this?" That would relieve Telan of their keep for more than half a year, while promising great rewards at their return. The Master in Verin would surely take them in that long.

"I care not where you take her as long as you leave this night and never return."

Rosher shook his head, stunned near into silence by that statement. "How will we survive?"

"That is your difficulty. If you will not abandon the Great Mage's spawn to whatever fate he makes for her, you will share her fate."

He looked to Riena, his stomach churning at the thought of leaving her to the winds of chance. "Nay," he whispered. "We will take what is ours and leave."

"Your clothing and nothing more."

"It is five days walk to the Master at Verin," Rosher protested.

"Mayhap her empty belly will still her hand."

Rosher bit back a curse at that and strode inside, collecting their clothing and boots into their cloaks under Belin's watchful eye. His gaze passed over sheets he could use as bandages for Riena. Rosher forced down his longing. No doubt he would sacrifice one of his own work tunics by morning to heal her. He left, a sour taste in his mouth at what was stolen from them. Rosher could feel his uncle's glare on his back deep into the field of flowers.

Chapter Two

Octen 24th, 4005

Riena looked up at the palace gates, her empty stomach rolling, scowling at Rosher's attempts to clean the road dust from her nose. "What if they turn us away?" she asked.

Winter was little more than a month off. Already, the nights were bitterly cold, and Riena huddled beneath Rosher's cloak with him to survive the night.

They'd made it this far by day-laboring for farms to fill their bellies, though the sunlight made her eyes water and her body weary. The season was ending, and no farm would hire on a permanent servant at this time of year. If the King refused them, as the Master Mage at Verin had, they were lost.

"They cannot," Rosher assured her, though his eyes were haunted in the shadow of his failure with the Master Mage. "If we beg an audience, they must hear us out."

Riena nodded stiffly. *But will they believe us and help? They are not required to do that.*

She looked to the approaching guard. It was a tall woman of about Rosher's height. Like all royal bodyguards, she was female—fast, strong, silent, and deadly protectors to the Mages who led them.

"What is your business?" the guard demanded.

Rosher sank to his knees, lowering his face in a sign of servitude. "We beg an audience, mi'lady."

Riena stood straight and tall, as Rosher told her she should. She was a Star Mage and should kneel only to a Mage her better.

The guard's gaze bored into her. "This ragged child knows not her place." She sneered.

"I know my place," Riena snapped. "I am a Star Mage in search of training."

The woman laughed. "You jest. There has not been a female Mage in more than a millennium."

Rosher took Riena's hand, mindful of her scars as always, stilling the protest gathering steam in her breast. "My sister is a Star Mage. I have seen her magic. Please, mi'lady. We must see His Majesty."

The guard nodded. "I warn you. If this is a trick, His Majesty will not be kind to you or your young charge." She opened the gate and waved them through, closing it carefully behind them.

The gardens were expansive, full of flowers Riena recognized—and many she didn't. Rosher hissed a warning when she reached for a blue flower she'd never seen before. Riena pulled her hand back, darkening at the reminder. These were not her flowers to handle, no matter how much she missed her circle.

"The girl will stay here until she is called for," the guard instructed.

"But how can His Majesty—" Rosher began.

"In due time. For now, he would see you alone." She glanced at Riena. "You may touch the flowers. The Trainee Mages will repair any damage you do." She led Rosher away before Riena could protest her assumption that there would be damage to repair.

The moon was peeking over the palace walls, the nearly full moon that sent tendrils of power coursing through her veins, though only Riena's face and hands were exposed to its rays. Riena touched the blue flower, inviting it to grow and smiling as its petals turned to her hand in thanks. So lost was she in her play that she didn't hear the boy approaching.

* * * *

Karris scowled at the girl. What was this filthy urchin doing in the royal gardens? From the dull hair that spoke of a week without soap and her threadbare cloak, he surmised she was the daughter of a widow here to beg winter employ from his father.

Every year, they came in droves, expecting his father to save them all. If that was their purpose, they'd wasted their trip. His father had taken on all he could two weeks earlier.

She didn't note his presence. The girl appeared deep in thought, her fingers stroking absently at the petals of the Blue Lady before her.

"Do not touch that flower," he snapped.

She jumped, looking to him, then to the Blue Lady. "The guard said—"

"I care not what the guard said." *The guard does not have to fix the damage. Master Caiben will make me repair it, and Blue Ladies are difficult to heal. That guard no doubt revels in the chance to make me do something I loathe, as all the guards seem to.* "Leave the gardens." *Better the chance that she will not cause me more practice this night.*

25

Her cheeks darkened past the already deep hue of the typical night-sleeper. "I was *ordered* to stay here."

Karris bristled at that. His annoyance grew as she stared into his face without any show of humility. "Who are you?"

"My name is Riena," she offered simply.

"Of what family?"

She hesitated. "I have only my brother, but his name is not mine to claim, since different men sired us."

Her hand returned to the Blue Lady, as if the texture soothed her. Blue Ladies were known for their delicate petals, delicate enough to tickle a Star Mage's tender hands, and so his father surrounded himself with them as many affluent Mages did.

"What of your mother?" he pressed her.

"Dead at my birth. Since both her family and my father's have forsaken me, I can claim no family."

Her shaking fingers bruised and creased the petals she touched. Karris cringed at that. It would take quite a bit of power to repair damage so deep. He pushed her away from the flower, grumbling a curse as the petals tore.

"I told you not to touch it," he complained, envisioning the lesson Master Caiben would serve him for this, the hour or more of meticulous release into the flower, until it showed no sign of abuse.

Riena stiffened. "Had you not pushed me," she shouted.

He rounded on her before she could finish her accusation. "Does being of no family cause this insufferable rude attitude, or is it your normal state of being?"

"Does being of a noble family cause yours?" she countered hotly.

Karris gaped at her. "Did no one ever teach you the proper address for your betters?"

Her eyes widened, searching over his clothing for any sign of his station and finding none, save the blue trim of the royal family. Her gaze passed over it without sign of recognition.

His father felt it beneath the "Vorian Heir" to wear the mark of his current rank, since all knew what color he would eventually wear, and so Karris wore no robes or sashes of Apprentice Purple that the girl might see.

"You are young to be a sealed Star Mage," she noted. "Have you completed your training yet?"

"Nay." He tried to keep the edge out of his voice at that. *Mother help me! Please, not another fool who believes only a sealed Mage is worthy of respect.* "But that—"

She sighed in relief. "Then you are not my better," she decided.

"Of course, I am," he exploded, cursing his lack of control over this situation. "Though I have not been tested at the Silver Minute—"

Riena threw back her head and laughed.

Karris glared at her. Black rage built within him. She was laughing at him. How dare she laugh at him! The blasted moon fed the force of his anger.

He smiled at the idea taking shape in his mind. Riena would learn her place. She would learn the power of a Star Mage, whether it be an Apprentice like himself or the king he would one day be.

Her laughter choked off on a startled cry as the thorn pierced her thumb, driving nearly through to the bone before Karris called a halt. Riena jerked her hand away from the bush, shooting him a look of surprise.

Karris shrugged, biting back a laugh of his own. "One should not taunt a Star Mage," he instructed her. "One never knows what his response may be to it."

Riena nodded, her eyes promising retribution she dared not seek. "Mayhap that is a lesson you need to learn better," she whispered.

He jerked as something surrounded his wrist, grinding his teeth against a scream of pain as the thorns bit deep. The stalk continued to grow, wrapping strands around his arm, points turned inward in mute warning.

Karris reined in his fear, soaking up the moon's radiance. The stalk halted at his command, then loosened. He met Riena's gaze as he ordered the plant to retreat. Her smug smile disappeared, and fear took its place. She looked to the stalk, no longer under her control, and bolted for the palace.

He nodded, pulling his bloodied hand free of her trap. "Run," he growled, "but you will not escape me."

* * * *

28

Rosher knelt, while King Etan stood beneath the moon, stripped to the waist and tending his fields with practiced ease.

The king sighed and turned to him. "And what boon do you seek?" he asked, as if weary of hearing petitions, though moonrise marked the beginning of a Mage's work. "If you have come seeking a place in service—"

"Nay, Majesty. I seek only training for my sister—and perhaps award of a bit of our dead mother's land that we might live."

"Training?" He looked to the guard who'd showed Rosher in. "What training does she seek, Reesa? As a bodyguard?"

Reesa bowed her head. "They say the child is a Star Mage," she offered in a voice that spoke her doubts.

Rosher winced at that. "She is a Mage. If you but test her— I beg only a proving. The Master at Verin would not—"

"Enough," King Etan ordered. He pulled a tunic over his lean body, brushing his dark hair away from whiskerless cheeks. He looked every bit the powerful Star Mage he was, fragile in form but housing a power that made burly men shake in fear.

"Has it come to this again?" he cursed.

"Pardon?" Rosher asked.

"I take it the girl was born on the night of the Grand Rebirth?"

Rosher nodded. "Ten years ago."

"At the Silver Minute?" he prodded.

"None can say."

The king looked back at him in surprise, his eyes narrowing. "Really?"

"Our mother died bringing Riena forth. She was dead, when we found them."

"What makes you believe your sister is a Star Mage then? If not the ancient stories about the girl born in the Silver Minute?"

"I have seen her magic. On the night of the Grand Rebirth past—"

"Impossible," the king snapped. "An untrained Mage cannot possibly survive such a channeling. It is a trick of some sort. Another Mage—"

"It was not," Rosher insisted. "You were not there to hear her screams, to see the sweat on her brow, to see the change move from her over the entire field."

"It cannot be."

"It injured her," he pleaded. "I tended the marks."

The king stilled, looking to the window, suppressing what appeared to be a shiver. "Describe them. These marks... What did they look like?"

"Burns on her hands, feet, and face. On all of her exposed flesh. It looked as if she stepped into a plume of steam. Her hands blistered the next morn."

He rubbed a hand over his smooth chin and looked to Reesa. "Her looks?" he asked quietly.

She scowled. "The child has the look of a Mage, but many children do. When a Star Mage finds solace in a local wench—"

"Her father was a Great Mage," Rosher offered. "Mayhap Riena's magic can be attributed to—"

"Which one?" the king interrupted him. "Which Great Mage sired her?"

"Great Mage Andren."

Reesa stepped toward him, her face twisted in fury. "Liar," she growled.

King Etan placed a hand on her arm to still her. "You should collect your sister and be on your way before I give Reesa leave to kill you both." His voice was as cold as his eyes.

Rosher's head spun. "You would cast out a young Mage to die in the coming winter?" If the king refused them, there was no hope of survival. "You would refuse her a proving?"

"You have been proven false," Reesa shouted.

"I told no falsehoods," he protested, sick at losing their last chance in so senseless a way.

"My father would never have forsaken my mother's memory that way."

"Your—"

"*My* father. When my mother died, he went on a pilgrimage to seek the Mother's rest. Half a year later, Andren was dead. He would not have lain with—" She took a deep breath, as if restraining herself from qualifying the wanton she believed Ellien to be.

"Mayhap he was weary and in need of a woman's hands. Mayhap he felt a kinship in that my mother was less than a year as a widow when Andren passed through. But never doubt that Ellien knew no other man to have sired Riena."

Reesa reached for her weapon. "You go too far."

"Then kill us now and quickly," he challenged. "It would save us the trouble of starving to death or freezing slowly." Rosher's heart pounded in terror at the thought that she might take him at his rash words and lay the blade in her hand to Riena's throat as she no doubt wished to.

For a hand of heartbeats, Reesa stared at him, seemingly shocked to silence by his demand for death.

Then Riena bolted through the open doorway, falling to her knees into his outstretched arms. She shook, looking to the doorway in undisguised fear.

"What is it?" Rosher asked, forgetting for a moment that Reesa intended to end his concern with the slice of her blade.

"A young Mage," she panted, wiping blood from her injured thumb on the skirt of her gown.

Rosher said a silent prayer that there was a second young Star Mage in the palace—that she'd not crossed the prince and sealed their fates. *Reesa did say the* Trainees *would repair any damage. There must be more than one.*

He shook his head at the sight of the young man in the tunic that matched the king's down to the star blue trim that signified the Royal house at the neckline. The sight of the blood streaming off the prince's hand made Rosher weary. There was no question that King Etan would give Reesa leave to kill them now—or worse.

"There you are," the prince growled at her. "You will learn not to attack me."

Rosher groaned.

"You attacked me *first*," Riena countered. "I have little training, but I know a Mage is not permitted to use his power against another unprovoked."

"I *was* provoked. You taunted me."

"Karris," the king barked. "You used your magic in anger?"

The prince darkened, flicking a look that promised a painful death at Riena. "She laughed at me," he grumbled.

King Etan crossed his arms over his chest, his gaze traveling to his son's blood-soaked hand. "A Star Mage who is ready for his seal, as you claim to be *so* vehemently, would be able to ignore something as petty as a taunt. I trust the girl pushed you into a thorn bush in response?"

Rosher flicked a look at Reesa. He wasn't certain the king's sympathy for Riena would save them. The look on the guard's face seemed to indicate that it wouldn't.

"Nay," Prince Karris stormed. "Nay, Father! The little beast used a Mage's powers against me. Dueling is—"

Etan motioned abruptly for silence.

Rosher breathed a sigh of relief at that. King Etan had heard it from his son's lips. Whether they believed who sired Riena or not, they knew he hadn't lied about her magic.

The king rubbed his smooth chin again, ranging his gaze over Riena. He ambled to them, grasping her hand and turning it palm up. Riena sank into Rosher's chest, barely breathing as King Etan examined the faint scars her blisters left. He rubbed his fingers over them, releasing her abruptly as Riena pulled her hand back in response. She shook, burying her sensitive hands in Rosher's tunic with a half-swallowed sob.

Rosher soothed her, keeping his gaze cast down so as not to show his disdain for the king that would do something he knew would hurt her. Riena was a child, and this maddening sensitivity was new to her. To play on it was cruel beyond words.

"The moon reaches its zenith in two hours," King Etan informed them. "Karris, have a healer tend to your wrist. Reesa...see to a room and food for our guests."

Rosher met his eyes in surprise.

The king nodded, then looked to Riena, his face searching hers as if some answer lay hidden in her dark eyes. "Rest well, young Mage. At the moon's zenith, you will have your proving." He left the room with a last look at Rosher that spoke of the price of failure.

* * * *

"Riena, the time has come."

Rosher shook her shoulder softly, dragging her from the depths of sleep. Riena opened her eyes, taking in his haggard appearance. Rosher hadn't slept. He couldn't sleep for sheer nervous energy, she knew. Riena only slept because she'd expended so much energy in attacking Prince Karris.

She placed a hand on his cheek, careful not to brush over his stiff whiskers. "I will not fail you," she promised.

His smile was strained. "I know."

Riena drank the tea Rosher offered and hurried to wash her face, but the king still seemed angry at her arrival.

He looked to the moon. "You are tardy," he informed her.

"My apologies," she answered, bowing her head. "I fell asleep."

The king raised an eyebrow at that. "You sleep the night?"

Karris snorted in half-suppressed laughter.

"We have had to day-labor to survive the trip," Rosher explained. "Though it is difficult for her, Riena has had no opportunity to sleep as befits a Star Mage."

She grimaced at that. Hoods to hide her skin from the rays of the sun had become essential to life.

"I see," he answered cryptically. "Very well. The plant you damaged, young Mage."

Riena shot a look at Karris that she hoped conveyed her loathing of him. The prince's smile grew, and he motioned to the broken flower with his bandaged hand.

She looked back to the flower, feeling her face heat in embarrassment. She hated admitting her failings in front of Karris, but there was no choice.

"I have never attempted a healing," she managed.

The king smiled and drew her hands to the flower, carefully avoiding her scars this time. "Encourage the damaged pieces to grow," he instructed. "That is all a healing is." His hands remained, cradling hers.

Riena looked to him fearfully.

35

"The flower," he reminded her.

She nodded, trying to concentrate on the flow of energy through her body, but the feeling of King Etan's hands unnerved her. Riena began to fear she might fail—until she caught sight of Karris's face.

His silent laughter mocked her. He *wanted* her to fail. It was a victory she would deny him with the last breath of her body.

Riena closed her eyes, remembering the feel of the petals between her fingers. The power flowed from her, and the king's gasp of surprise stirred her hair. She ignored it, urging the flower to grow and be strong.

A tremendous cracking sound intruded on her thoughts, and Riena opened her eyes, watching the bush exploding in growth in mounting dismay. "Nay," she pleaded, trying to pull her hands back.

The king held them in place, his hands clamped tight around her wrists. "Concentrate," he ordered.

She continued with a sob. No matter how she tried to bend the magic to make the flowers heal, the bush grew larger. It finally blocked the moon's light, casting shadows over her. The power rushing through her diminished to a trickle.

Riena sank to her knees, tears streaming down her face. "Please," she begged. "I can do better. I swear I can."

"Better?" the king asked.

"The task was to heal," she whispered. She'd failed. Riena had caused growth instead. Would King Etan turn them away?

He knelt to the ground next to her, holding a flower plucked from the bush. "Look at it," he invited her.

Riena wiped her tears on the cuff of her gown and took the blue flower from him. She stared at it without comprehension, then looked to him, hoping he would explain his point.

"This was your flower, young Mage." His long, slim fingers stroked her cheek. "Your healing was flawless, but you lack control in stopping the flow of energy. Training will solve that."

She nodded, her mind numb in exhaustion.

"This land you want?" he prodded her, tracing the line of her brow and nose.

The soothing motion made thinking more difficult. "My flowers. I want my flowers."

The king looked to the bush in confusion, perhaps wondering if she was asking for the precious plant to be given to her.

Riena shook her head. "*My* flowers."

"The flowers Great Mage Andren created for our mother," Rosher explained quietly. "Riena was conceived there and born there. She faced the Silver Minute there. It is her special place."

He nodded in understanding. "When you faced the Silver Minute, did you make the flowers grow?" he asked.

She glanced at Rosher, grimacing at his look of pain. "Nay," she breathed. "I—I destroyed the harvest."

The king's smile disappeared. His face lost what little color it had naturally. "Destroy? A Star Mage's magic cannot destroy."

37

"A man can live on grain. He cannot feed on flowers, like the sweet songbirds do."

Rosher's hand closed on her shoulder. "Riena is untrained, Majesty. She did not *intend* to turn the crops into a field of her flowers."

"She transformed them?" he asked, his tone urgent, as if such a thing were of paramount importance. "She did not simply cause the flowers to overgrow the grain and choke it out?"

Riena nodded miserably.

King Etan stood and helped Riena to her feet. "Come. There is much to discuss."

"There is?" Rosher asked, steadying Riena as he guided her toward the palace.

"There is indeed. I would like Master Jerin to instruct her first. I trust him to teach Riena the proper control for a magic so strong. Control will be very important to you, young Apprentice."

Riena gasped at that. She had expected to be called a Trainee, but mayhap her premature seal prevented him from naming her at a beginner's level. Were she not so confused by the speed of things, she might have asked him that question, along with a hundred others pouring through her still-muddled mind.

"In the meantime," he continued, as if she hadn't made a sound, "I will correct your misstep with the crops."

Rosher laughed, a nervous, high-pitched sound that announced his giddy disbelief. "My thanks. Grandfather will appreciate that."

"The family Karris tells me has abandoned her?" King Etan asked pointedly.

"Yes, but—"

"They will have land, but not the land I will restore. That land is for yourself and Riena."

"You give us too much," Rosher noted, his eyes wild.

Riena shivered at the reaction their family would have to being thrown from their land for her. "Grandfather will—"

"After tonight, your grandfather will dare not harm you," the king informed her.

"Because I am a Star Mage?" she asked in confusion. There were laws about harming a Mage, but the laws could only do so much.

King Etan turned to them, his smile the widest Riena had seen from him yet. His eyes glittered in the moonlight. "Nay, Apprentice Riena. Because I claim a King's Right."

Rosher's hands tightened on her shoulders. Riena watched as his face went a sickly gray shade. Though she wasn't familiar with the term, Riena felt chilled by her brother's response to it.

"Father," Karris protested. "You cannot do this."

"I can and I have." The king shot his son a look of warning. "You will comply with my wishes, Karris."

"But she is—"

"A female of my realm of extraordinary power, Karris. She will take her place, and you will accept that."

"You cannot—"

Etan made a noise of warning, his face hard in decision. Karris broke off, sending a look that promised pain and suffering at Riena before he stormed to the palace without a backward glance.

From somewhere in the distance, the sound of breaking glass jangled along Riena's nerves. Then all was silent.

"I do not understand," she managed shakily.

The king laughed heartily. "It means you are legally my child," he explained.

"Your daughter?" she asked, warmed by the idea of being a princess—or mayhap by the idea that King Etan wanted her to be his daughter.

"Not yet. When you reach your twentieth year, you will take my heir as mate."

Riena's stomach wrestled with the tea Rosher gave her to drink before her test. She looked to the palace in understanding. "Karris?" she squeaked. It was no wonder that he was furious with her.

"Of course."

Rosher scooped her up as Riena's balance deserted her, following the oblivious King Etan into his home. Her head spun lightly as His Majesty ordered her life for years to come.

Chapter Three

Marz 20th, 4015

Riena stood at the window of what was once her mother's rooms, watching the messenger from Etan take to his horse and leave with a bow of his head her direction. She fisted the drape, then let it fall, cursing the brush burns she'd left on her tender skin.

Rosher's knock was enthusiastic. "Riena," he called.

"I do not wish to see it," she replied miserably.

He sighed. "May I enter?"

"Please." Rosher was still her only friend, the only one who loved her. She sighed. He would likely always be, even when she fulfilled the damned decree and took Karris as her mate.

Rosher waited patiently for her to turn. He smiled in encouragement when she did. "He sends you so many wonderful things," he pointed out to her.

"Nay. Etan sends them. Not Karris," she assured him.

"How can you know that?"

She didn't know it for certain, but Riena wouldn't admit that. "We have met him. How can you question it?"

"Nay, Riena. We met a stubborn thirteen-year-old boy who had just been bested by an untrained girl three years his junior. His pride was injured—and his wrist. How can you know what changes a decade have made in him?"

41

She couldn't. Mother take all the men who ordered her life! "Karris did not want this mating, Rosher. He does not even know me."

"He could. He asks with every messenger he sends. At least once a week he asks, and you turn him away. Do you want to mate with a stranger, Riena?"

Her stomach twisted painfully at that. "I do not wish to mate at all," she admitted.

Rosher smiled an indulgent smile. "Fear speaks for you. I have heard it said that a Mage's mating is beyond any mating I could compare it to of my own experience. Your sensitivity—"

"Does his messenger tell you that?" she countered. "Mayhap Karris wants a more biddable woman in his bed than he anticipates with me. Mayhap he wishes you to calm me for him."

She winced at his look of shock. "I am sorry, Rosher. Yes. My fear speaks for me. Not of mating," she was quick to assure him. Mating was a biological function. There should be nothing to fear in that. If facing the Silver Minute didn't kill her, what was there to fear in this?

"Of mating with Karris," he guessed.

"With any man not of my choosing." She started pacing the room, rubbing her hands up and down her arms to still the chillbumps rising under her gown.

"Meet with him and see if you could love him," Rosher urged her.

"Nay. I cannot. I would be a fool in his sight. I know it. He is trained to exploit the weaknesses of his adversaries."

"You believe he would stoop to that?" he asked in seeming amazement.

Riena rubbed at the scar on her thumb, not meeting his gaze

"He was a boy," Rosher protested.

"A boy with an advantage. Now he is a man with a greater advantage."

Riena didn't have to say more. She'd been denied half of her training by Etan. In an effort to make her dependant on her "mate," the king had decreed that only Karris could complete her training—the very night she took up residence in her Master Jerin's home.

Had she the training she lacked, Riena might have proven what she'd believed all along. She might have proven that there was a way to avoid this mating. There were too many questions the Master Mages wouldn't answer, too many guarded looks that spoke of things Riena should know but they were not permitted to teach her.

The only thing that was certain was that Etan had the right to demand King's Right of any exceptional woman in his kingdom. Riena wasn't certain what in Mage's law might nullify that. Perhaps there was nothing, and she had simply dreamed an escape for herself all these years.

Rosher wrapped his arms around her, drawing Riena to his chest. "The King's Right is unbreakable. If I could, I would break it for you. You know that I would."

"I know." She sighed. "What has Karris sent me this time?" Mayhap it was best to simply ask what waited her.

"Mage's robes. Heavy winter robes and light summer ones..." He hesitated, burying his face in her hair.

"What is it?"

"One of them is to be your mating robe."

Riena groaned at the thought. Asking was decidedly not better.

* * * *

Riena stood before the mirror, surveying the mating robe. It was exquisite star blue silk, trimmed in silver. She ran her hands down her stomach, gasping at the feel of the silk cascading over her naked body. Her nipples beaded against the material, and she moaned at the thought of wearing this gown.

The memory of Etan's hands cupping hers raced through her mind. The king had always been gentle with her, save that first touch of his hands over her sealing scars. He'd always been considerate of her sensibilities, except where the King's Right was concerned. What would those hands that cradled hers have felt like on her body?

She shook her head at that. Nay. Etan was nearly her father's age, more the parent she'd never had than a lover. Still, her senses were strangely aroused by the robe.

Riena raised the hood, covering her black braid with the blue material. Yes. There was a faint scent clinging to the silk, a scent that sent curls of pleasure through her.

Her eyes in the mirror caught her attention. Other eyes flashed into her mind—black eyes like hers that were hot in emotion. What would those eyes look like when heated in passion instead of fury? What would Karris—

Riena gasped, shocked at the path her mind had taken. What trick was this that she was lusting after *Karris*?

She started to push the hood down, then stilled, staring at the reflected image in momentary confusion. Riena rushed to the dresser, pulling down her hood and taking up the jeweled dagger Karris had sent her weeks earlier. She sliced off her braid at halfway down her neck and dropped it to the dresser with the dagger, running her hands through her hair to muss it as she returned to the mirror.

Riena stifled a laugh of glee. It would work. A few more touches, and she would convince Rosher of the plan.

* * * *

Rosher squinted into the weak Terra Set sunlight, taking in the strange Star Mage in his doorway in surprise. He sat up, rubbing the sleep from his eyes and focusing blearily on the black robe that announced a Master Mage.

"My pardons," he yawned. "It is day, Master. Can I arrange a place for you to sleep?"

Riena's laughter teased at his ears.

He forced his eyes to focus on the Mage, swallowing a curse. "Riena, why are you awake? It must be nearly high day. You— By the Mother Moon!"

Rosher jumped from the bed, fingering her hair in dismay.

"What have you done?" he demanded.

She darkened but didn't answer. Her hair was chin-length around, in the style of a young Mage with his seal. Riena wore a heavy winter cloak in the place of a robe, but at a distance, it was indistinguishable.

He swore aloud at the flat plane of her chest. "You bound your breasts."

"Men do not have them," she reasoned.

"You cannot pass for a man," he argued.

"A man like you? Nay. I cannot. A Star Mage? Why should it be difficult? All Mages have feminine features. They do not grow facial hair, have black hair in a style such as this, and have dark eyes like mine. Why should anyone question that I am what I appear to be?"

"You have the mannerisms of a woman." *Please, Mother! Tell me she is playing some sort of prank and not suggesting this in earnest.*

"Teach me. You are a man, though not a Star Mage. Teach me to present the appearance of a man."

"Why are you doing this?"

She shifted nervously. "I do not wish to mate, Rosher. You promised to help me if there were a way to escape the King's Right. I have longed to run for so many years, but there was never a way to hide that I am a Mage. I do not have to hide it. Do you see? I only have to hide that I am female. You know me better than anyone, and I fooled you at first glance." Her eyes pleaded with him, heartbreakingly hopeful.

Still Rosher hesitated. If they were caught—

"I never chose him," she choked out. "Please, do not ask me to take a mate I have not chosen."

His heart ached at that. Rosher couldn't ask it. He'd never thought it was fair to force this on her. "If we are caught, Etan will have no mercy," he warned her.

She nodded stiffly. "Then we must not be caught."

Rosher grumbled his agreement, and Riena threw herself into his arms with a squeal of joy.

"Lesson one, Riena. Men do not show such outward signs of thanks. Lesson two; men do not squeal like little children."

She nodded enthusiastically. "I will remember that."

* * * *

Marz 24th, 4015

"But why can I not sit *this* way?" Riena asked for the third time, her right knee still hooked over the left and her foot swinging lightly.

Rosher rolled his eyes. "Because a man would not. Do you wish people to know you for a woman or to believe you a man?" This would fail if she fought him at every step.

"I saw Nuvan sit like this only a few weeks ago in town." She smiled in perceived victory.

"Then you wish to advertise that you favor the company of other men?" he asked patiently.

47

Riena's eyes opened wide. She dropped her foot to the floor with a shake of her head.

"Good," he decided, rubbing his forehead with his fingertips. Who knew teaching a woman to act like a man could be so difficult?

"That really means..." she began carefully.

"Yes, it does. It will be difficult enough keeping women away from a young Mage. I would prefer not to have to dissuade men, as well."

"What will we do about the women?"

"I will have to sleep on the floor, I suppose."

"You could share my bed," she offered.

Rosher raised an eyebrow.

"Oh. I suppose that would be apparent."

"It would to an observant matron."

"And that would entice the men?" she guessed.

He nodded.

Riena sighed. "This is impossible."

A traitorous corner of Rosher's mind urged him to agree. Life with Karris couldn't possibly be worse than the punishment if they were caught.

Then he remembered Riena's tears when the first gift had arrived from Karris. She hadn't wanted this life. Riena was a person—not to be dismissed as the rest of her family had dismissed her and not to be traded as property.

He took her hands. "Not impossible but difficult. Surely, it is not too difficult for a sealed Star Mage to manage."

Riena smiled at him with eyes misted in tears. She nodded, then took a calming breath. "Then teach me how a man would sit."

* * * *

Marz 30th, 4015

"Nay, Riena," Rosher protested. "You are too powerful. No one would believe you are less than a Mason. Mayhap they would expect you to be a Master Mage."

"With my lack of training, I cannot risk presenting as a Mason. If there would not be questions of who my Master was, I would present as an Apprentice."

He groaned at the complexity of it. Rosher grudgingly accepted her assertion that her robes would have to be green Midman robes, cut from the three green gowns she owned, the scraps burned in the fire as her hair and all other proof had been. Knowing Master Jerin had raised her to Mason—still a lesser rank than she deserved to hold, it rankled Rosher to see her accept a lesser rank.

"You will make less money as a Midman," he reminded her, grasping at a last effort to sway her to Mason brown.

"I will make a reputation over time. One poor season will make me known as worth my keep."

"Making a reputation is dangerous, Riena."

She fumbled, piercing her scarred thumb with the needle. Riena stared into the flames, her breathing hard and the green fabric fisted in her hands.

"Riena?" he asked.

"I die either way, Rosher. I die a slave to Etan and Karris, or I die a free Star Mage." Her voice was little more than a growl.

Rosher knelt to her, caressing her cheek, soothing her by touching the sensitive flesh that proved what she was. "That was the voice of a man. You are ready."

Riena looked to her sewing, resuming her work in earnest. "Not yet," she breathed, "but soon."

* * * *

Marz 32nd, 4015

"No, Rosher." Riena pulled the pack he'd stocked apart. She should have realized he would pack as he usually did for a trip to Master Jerin, save the difference in clothing.

"What is wrong with it?" he asked, his brow furrowed in confusion.

She tossed the soap onto her bed. "A common Mage would not own such finery. A simple sage soap will suffice."

Rosher darkened at his mistake, then nodded. "The scent would draw attention," he conceded.

"It would." A small pack of jewels landed next to the soap.

His eyes widened. "We may need to trade with those," he protested. "What we leave is lost forever."

"How did we come by them? What noble family have we stolen from? I can claim no noble family—even the one that is truly mine."

Rosher winced at that.

"I cannot take these things, Rosher. They were given in trust of a mating that will never come to pass. They are Karris's. The coin I earned is my own. It will have to suffice."

"And if it does not?"

She shook her head, burying her uncertainties. "I do not know," she admitted. Mayhap Etan would show Rosher mercy, if she surrendered herself to Karris. Riena would hope for Etan's mercy. Karris's mercy was an uncertain thing.

Rosher's hands closed around her shoulders. "Do not doubt yourself."

"I should not do this, Rosher."

"It is your life."

"And yours," she countered. "It will go worse for you than for me."

"Will it?" he asked.

Riena hesitated. It would. Surely, Rosher knew that.

"When Etan turned us away, I asked for our deaths."

She looked up sharply, tears clouding her eyes. "Nay! Oh, Rosher! You didn't."

He nodded.

"How could you do such a thing?" she screamed at him, stifling the urge to strike him. If she did, she would only harm herself.

Rosher brushed her tears away tenderly. "A quick death," he whispered. "It was that or watching you starve, mayhap finding you lost to the winter cold one morning."

"But—"

He pressed his fingertips to her lips, shaking his head. "Should I die quickly, Riena? Or should I watch you die a night at a time, tied to a man you do not love?"

Riena swallowed a lump in her throat and nodded, fresh tears spilling down her cheeks.

"Then we leave in three days," he reminded her.

"Thank you, Rosher."

She could never repay him for the sacrifices he made for her. It would have been so easy for him to agree to let her give up hope, along with her chance for freedom. Could she do the same? If it meant his life, she thought she might.

* * * *

Abrin 3rd, 4015

"Can we stop yet?" Riena pleaded. "We have come far into the mountains."

Rosher cupped her cheeks in both of his hands, meeting her unfocused gaze. "I know day travel is difficult..." he began.

"My eyes water, Rosher. I am tired. It has been half a day." She weaved on her feet.

He winced at that. They'd set out at moonset to draw the least amount of attention. No one would expect a Star Mage to travel by day.

But now it was high day, and Riena was exhausted. Tears streamed down her face from the sting of the sun she hadn't faced fully in a decade. Her pale skin, a sign of her lifestyle, was pink in reaction to the rays that barely supported crops.

Rosher looked around cautiously. "No one is about," he decided.

"Then we can make camp?" she asked hopefully.

"Nay. We cannot."

She groaned as if in agony.

He turned and knelt to offer her his back. "Climb on," he ordered.

"I do not—" Her voice was thick, and her hand trembled against his shoulder.

"I will carry you as I did when you were a child."

Riena questioned him no further. She settled on his back, her arms wrapped around his shoulders and her legs hooked over his forearms.

She wasn't as light as she had been when she was ten, but if it meant their continued freedom, Rosher would willingly carry Riena every day while she slept and sleep every night while she earned their food.

Chapter Four

Abrin 7th, 4015

Karris sighed, pulling the laces on his boots tight. "She ran."

He didn't have to question it. The fury on Lena's face told him all he needed to know. Karris sent up thanks to Mother Moon that he'd decided to start sending messengers to her twice weekly. Had he not, her departure might not have been discovered for another four days.

"Coward," Lena spat, her hand laid over the hilt of her dagger.

"Nay, Lena. Riena was very brave to try this." If his father caught her, the king could kill both of them for balking King's Right. Even if Etan wanted to follow through with this madness, Rosher would be killed to guarantee he couldn't aid Riena in escape again.

Karris winced at that. Etan would kill Rosher and force Riena to Karris's bed. The Mages would rise up if he dared execute one of the precious female Star Mages. They barely held violence in sway for Etan's decision to force her to King's Right. Killing her would push them too far.

Etan had chosen this course out of fear for his throne. Binding Riena to his house was the only way he could ensure her alliance without causing civil war over the issue.

She'd been taught by those loyal to Etan, Masters who wouldn't dream of reporting all of his crimes to the Great Houses. As long as it appeared Riena was willing to submit to the mating— As long as no one outside the palace knew she'd been denied knowledge of her true rights, Etan was safe from reprisals. That meant Etan had to follow this course to the end.

Nay. Etan would kill Rosher, despite the fact that Riena would hate them both for it. It would be kinder to kill Riena outright than to make her live with the loss of her brother.

An image of the child Riena had been, huddled in her brother's arms in Etan's throne room, tortured him. He took to his feet, determined to save that precious bond. Had he ever truly doubted it would come to this?

"What will you do?" Lena asked.

Karris strode to his cabinets with his far-removed cousin at his heels. "I will find her—personally."

That was the only chance Riena and Rosher had, though they surely had no idea that it was true. Karris would find her. He had to be the one to find Riena, because no one else would guarantee her rights.

As much as my father allows, he reminded himself. There were some things he could not remedy until he was king.

Lena chuckled, a dark sound that proved she had no understanding of Karris's true purpose. With her trained dislike of Riena, Lena would envision him tracking her down and ordering Rosher's death while he took what was his by King's Right. Karris swallowed a sour lump at that thought. It would never pass that way. No matter what he had to do to stop it, he would never claim Riena in so barbaric a fashion.

His bags were packed and hidden in the back corner of his cabinet. Karris collected them and headed for the stables. He'd known this was coming. He'd planned for it, praying every moonset that Riena would relent and let him come to her, that she wouldn't force them both to this course. Her mistrust ran too deep for that, as Karris had feared it would.

Etan appeared as Karris mounted his horse. "How many will accompany you?" he asked.

Karris raised the hood of his blue robes, shadowing his face and hiding the tense line of his jaw. "Only Lena. This is my grievance and no one else's."

"I expect you to—"

"I know my duty, Father. I will not execute Riena to win my freedom."

Karris didn't bother to mask his sarcasm. Etan would expect him to be sour at the thought of bringing Riena home as his mate. His father had never understood his objections—or rather, he'd chosen to pretend he didn't.

"Protect him well, Lena."

She bowed her head to Etan, then to her mother, Reesa. Karris sighed deeply as he left the palace grounds behind.

Lena's presence complicated matters, no doubt the reason Etan had her assigned to Karris to begin with. Etan would stand for nothing less than a Great house An bodyguard in this case. They were the best bodyguards in service. That much was true, and so it was not unexpected that the Vorian Heir would travel with nothing less, but the An guards also loathed the possibility that

Riena was of their blood and would make certain she paid a high price for balking Etan.

"To her home?" Lena asked briskly.

"Any good search would start there."

It took them almost a full moonrise to reach the house, with its orchards, fields, and gardens.

Karris left Lena to their horses while he searched for clues. Riena left no doubt to her intentions. All of the gifts Karris had sent were laid neatly over her bed, even the ones he'd believed she would use to facilitate her escape.

He furrowed his brow at that. She'd taken none of the coins and jewels he sent, not the dagger, not even the light-blocking fabric that might save her tender skin harm if she found herself outside during the light of day.

Her cabinets were full of dresses that appeared nearly untouched and her brown Mason's robes. Even her bath was fully stocked with soaps and salts. Had she left with nothing but the clothes on her back, a bit of food, and Rosher? That seemed unlikely.

Karris knelt to her bedside, drawing in Riena's scent. That scent had haunted him for months, brought to him on letters in her hand, letters where Riena refused to see him. All he had of her were memories of a dirty-faced child with fury in her eyes, that scent, and descriptions from his messengers of a sad beauty who stole the breath away.

He fingered the silk mating robes, smiling to himself weakly. The robes held a trace of her scent. Had she worn them, or had they picked up the fragrance from the bed? He furrowed his brow at another scent, an elusive scent that hinted at memories he couldn't quite grasp.

Karris stood with the silk in his hands, drawing that scent deep into his lungs. He dropped the robes with a muttered curse on his father.

These things had been from Karris. Etan had no right to tamper with them. Had the aphrodisiac effect of the Blue Lady nectar offended her? Mayhap frightened her? There was no way to know until he found her. Karris prayed he wouldn't find her too late to make this right.

Lena was waiting for him downstairs. "How did she escape?" she asked. "With our men watching the roads, how could she?"

Karris glanced at the view through the window, considering that. "Through the orchard and over the mountains. It would have been the only way."

"Then we can reach them at Ber or Verin. They cannot be much further unless they purchased mounts."

"Nay. They left everything of value behind."

Lena was silent for a long moment. "She cannot hide for long. The moon reaches its second crest in a week. Even if she hides her skin—"

He nodded. "I know." How did Riena intend to hide it? Karris sighed, certain that she had a plan, though he couldn't fathom what it might be.

"The moon will set soon. Fetch supplies in town. Remember not to use my name. We sleep here tonight. It is time to don my disguise."

She scowled at that, much as she had when Karris had explained his plan on the trip to Riena's home. "Is this really necessary, Karris?"

"My presence causes a stir. Riena would be well away before I reached her."

"But a Master? Really, cousin! At least a Great Mage—"

"Would draw attention I do not wish. A Master Mage is common, and common is what I must be." Karris rubbed the tension from the base of his skull. "It is my wish to locate Riena quickly. Please, Lena. Please, do as I wish."

"Your father will not approve," she warned him.

"I know it, but sacrifices must be made to reach our goals. My father would not approve if I lost track of Riena much more."

Lena bowed her head slightly and strode away. Karris just hoped she wouldn't wake some poor shopkeep before the moon was nearly set and the night-sleepers stirring. His cousin often lacked patience, another detriment to his cause.

Karris set about making a fire in the hearth, his mind buzzing. What was Riena's plan? How could she hope to hide what she was? It seemed an impossible task. Any trained Mage in the area would feel her releases of power, and one could never be certain when a Mage would be near.

He stilled, poking at a flash of color in the ash, then pulling it free. It was a bit of green-dyed wool. Karris stared into the ashes as if they held all the answers he sought. Mayhap they did, but the cold hearth held its secrets well.

* * * *

Abrin 8th, 4015

Karris added a small pack to his horse's cargo bags, smoothing the black robes that announced him as a Master Mage. His own robes had been left with Riena's everynight robes in her room. Only a single sash of prince's blue would travel with him, hidden deep in his packs.

He'd chosen to sleep in her bed the day before. There were two rooms that were blocked of light for the use of Mages. There was no reason for Karris to torture himself with her scent while he should have rested, no reason but that he never realized how much he would miss that scent when there was every possibility that he would never know its like again. Being surrounded by it was comforting, giving him hope that he would succeed in his search.

Riena shouldn't have been forced to this extreme. His father had been wrong to use King's Right against another Mage. The two were at odds with each other.

True, King's Right gave Etan power to demand any woman he found extraordinary for his heir's mate, but it was an ancient, underused law from the time of the first Great Mages. Mages' law, as set out in *The Master's Words*, was specific.

A female Mage was rare and precious. The choice of mate was hers to make. The one she approached as mate and took to her bed would share a power when soulbound that could bring prosperity or wreck destruction on the face of Terra Set.

It was that possibility that made Etan do something so foolhardy, the possibility that Riena would choose another and choose to soulbind with him, a lesser Mage with aspirations of power at any cost.

Their own house had taken the throne in such a manner when the last female Star Mage had mated into their family. For all that he presented the face of a strong king, Etan was a coward afraid of losing his position by virtue of the strength of that mating. Karris knew it to be true, though Etan always claimed simply to want the novelty of such a beautiful and gifted bride for his son.

Then Etan had gone one step further, compounding his crime. He'd decreed that Riena's training be sacrificed to keep her ignorant of her rights as a Mage. She would not know how completely she'd been wronged until she was tied to Karris as her mate.

For almost half his life, Karris had protested this course of action. Etan persisted in his belief that his son simply resisted being ordered to mate at his father's whim. Karris supposed it was easier for Etan to believe that than to face his son's condemnation for his very real crimes.

Be mindful of the limitations of your power. Master Caiben had taught Karris that. He'd repeated it, most likely at Etan's urging, every moonrise from the night Riena entered his life until Karris won his seal and surpassed his master.

He fingered the leather braceband that covered the scars Riena had gifted him during their duel. She was strong. She'd always been strong.

"Karris?" Lena's voice was laced with concern, making him wonder how many times she'd called him before he realized it.

"Yes, Lena?"

"Are you well?"

He mounted his horse and turned toward the moonlit orchard. "I am well," he lied.

Karris headed off in chase of the woman he would love to set free. There were worse things than being found by Karris, and he would do anything to spare her those things.

* * * *

Abrin 18th, 4015

"I do not understand it," Lena complained bitterly. "It is almost as if she ceased to exist when she walked away."

Karris nodded, barely keeping his mount beneath him in his exhaustion. "We must stop." His heart ached at that, at abandoning his quest for another day.

Every night was the same. They set off at moonrise, searching all night, questioning night-sleepers until they retired to their rest and again at moonset, until Karris could stand the day no longer.

Lena dismounted, helping Karris down as if he were a child and easing him to a patch of soft grass. He rested while she raised his tent, hidden beneath the folds of the cloak he'd lined with light-blocking cloth, beaten, discouraged, confused at his complete failure.

He'd expected to find her by now, but they'd learned nothing. Ber and Verin both yielded no information. There were drifting farm workers passing through, some groups with women but always grandmothers or mothers, gravid or with nursing young.

Karris had pushed on to Dray and Cerse. His hopes had been raised. There was a man and woman who traveled together. Both were reported to be fair-haired, but changing Riena's appearance was to be expected. It had taken them three nights to track the pair, but it wasn't Riena and her brother. Their skin was stained by years of night-sleeping, not milky white as Mother Moon.

Lena shouldered him up, half carrying Karris to his pallet and closing him into the blackness his body craved. Through the light-blocking walls, he could hear her pitching her own tent and tending to their animals.

He groaned. How was Riena hiding? The second crest had come and gone with no sign of her.

She is powerful, he reminded himself. *Riena is brilliant, mayhap more brilliant than anyone anticipated of her.*

Chapter Five

Abrin 19th, 4015

"Should you not disrobe, young Midman?" the woman called, her eyes hungry.

Riena bit back a scowl at that. It was almost always the same. Farmers mistrusted her, and their unmated adult daughters wished to bed her, believing Riena male.

In truth, their fathers probably wished the same. A trained Star Mage, conceived in such a joining, was Mother-sent and at his family's whims from onset of power to maturity. Better, the Mage who took such a daughter to mate brought the guarantee of prosperity and extra coin.

It was so universal that Riena had begun to thank the Mother every time she served a house with no such daughters. This was not one of those nights.

"Young Midman," she called again. "Should you not disrobe?"

"Nay," Riena replied calmly. "It is not necessary."

"I am paying for your best, young Mage," the farmer snapped at her.

Riena glared at him. "Mother Moon's light is strong tonight. You will be satisfied with the channeling."

"If I am not—" He took a step toward her.

Rosher moved to intercept him, his eyes hard. "You will not be if you interrupt Midman Romik's concentration much more," he growled. "Mages speak of such things, Farmer Zon."

He let the threat hang between them.

The farmer looked to Riena fearfully. The threat of no Mage willingly serving his land when he had need was usually an effective tool. This time was no different.

Zon bowed his head and backed off two paces. "My apologies, Midman Romik. It is just this blight..."

Riena nodded. It was true. The blight on the local crops had many farmers out of sorts. She had seen it well. What surprised her was that Zon had been the first to trust her to attempt a healing. One would think that the farmers would grasp at any chance offered to safeguard their interests, but they didn't.

She closed her eyes, finding focus in the rising moon, curling her toes in the soft soil. Riena raised her hands in offering to the Mother, baring her face and neck to the night lights.

She hadn't lied. The moon was strong. The power raced along Riena's skin, caressing her cheek as Master Jerin's hands once had, as Rosher did to soothe her.

Her body responded as it always did, her nipples tightening and aching at the power's touch, her womb becoming hot and heavy in excitement. It was no wonder that Mages took the farmers' daughters so often in the aftermath of a channeling. It was no wonder that Mages chose to soulbind if their mates were willing.

She wondered briefly what climax in the Silver Minute would be like—then forced her mind back to her work. It had been two lean days. This channeling had to go well.

It would be difficult. Healing shade rot was draining, but Riena's healing was said to be unequalled. She hoped it was true.

The power surged within her. Riena let it build until the itch was near maddening, releasing it slowly and carefully into the crops around her. She pushed herself hard, making the most of the magic in fierce determination. Their future depended on her proving herself, on Midman Romik making a name for himself with these farmers.

When she was depleted, Riena collapsed into Rosher's arms, accepting a bottle of water with unsteady hands. He sat with her, tending to Riena's needs while Farmer Zon inspected his crops, moving plant to plant with a stunned look. As if he feared some trick, he motioned his sons to other corners of the field. Riena stifled a growl at that, at the mistrust that was like a wall between the farmers and Star Mages.

Zon turned to them, thoughtful, stroking a healthy leaf between his big fingers. "You did well. There is no sign of rot, and you speeded our harvest by more than a week."

Riena nodded. "I must sleep, Farmer Zon."

"Sleep, young Mage. Mayhap, when you recover, you would consider doing the same for my brothers' fields?"

"A week," Rosher demanded, looking up from her boot laces. "Midman Romik will need a week to perform another channeling so difficult."

"Done. And a bonus of another ten silver, if their harvests speed as well."

Riena stood on uncertain legs, weaving in Rosher's embrace. The house seemed too far, her legs stiff and unfeeling.

"You push too far," Rosher whispered.

"I will not fail you."

* * * *

Mey 5th, 4015

Rosher ground his teeth in frustration as Riena healed her third field in as many weeks. Their purse was heavy enough to support them for most of a winter already, and there was still more than half a growth cycle to work. It was time to start insisting that Riena let him use the surplus to purchase essentials: light-blocking cloth, a decent tent, mayhap even horses. She pushed too hard with too few personal comforts.

They were promised three more days keep and two weeks of food on leaving. It was the perfect time to buy what she needed to be comfortable—if she let him do so. She had made a name. Riena could rest now, but she was driven not to fail him.

He grumbled at that, at the truth that he could do nothing to ease her burden, while Riena cared for them both. She saw it as a labor of love in repayment for the years Rosher had raised her. Riena argued that it was her turn to provide. None of that made Rosher feel better.

Riena staggered, landing on her knees, her trembling severe. Rosher stroked her chilled cheek, holding the water for her as she drank her fill, then easing her boots on.

In the field, Farmer Zon clapped his youngest brother on the shoulder. "Did we not tell you he was worth his weight in coin?"

"That you did, Brother."

Rosher caught the damned bag of coin tossed carelessly at Riena. The fool would have struck her with it were Rosher not so swift of hand, but she wouldn't thank him for pointing that out to the careless oaf.

"Sleep well, Midman Romik. You are welcome next year. Very welcome, indeed."

Riena buried her face in Rosher's shoulder, feeling the effects of the channeling, no doubt weary to her bones. He helped her to her feet, steadying Riena as they entered the stand of trees that stood between the planting fields and the room she needed so desperately.

"Greetings, Midman Mage," a voice called out.

Rosher stilled, seeking out the shadowed forms before them. He edged back, sensing something sinister in their appearance, though bandits would seldom trouble a Star Mage. The penalties for such a thing were simply too high.

"Leaving?" The new voice came from behind them.

"What do you want?" Riena asked weakly.

The first man spoke again. "You will find that more experienced Mages do not care for young travelers like yourself taking the coin from our purses."

Rosher prayed she'd hold her tongue. If Riena pointed out their inability or unwillingness to end this blight, they were as good as dead in an illegal duel.

She didn't disappoint him. "You wish me to go elsewhere next year?" she asked.

The third man broke his silence. "Star Mages know respect for a Mage who serves his time before wandering," he suggested smoothly.

Riena shuddered against him, and Rosher bit back a groan. There was no possibility of Riena doing that. She couldn't hide what she was through three years of service...or more. Riena couldn't even promise to do it in order to win their freedom. Mages spoke about such things.

"Midman Mage," the first prodded her.

She shook her head. "Nay. With all respect, Brother Mage, I will not serve in that way."

Rosher counted the breaths in the silence that followed. They are Mages, he calmed himself. Their own laws and the laws of Voria decree that they cannot press the issue further.

"You will not reconsider?" he asked carefully.

Riena moved closer to Rosher. "Nay. I cannot in good conscience tell you that I would."

The Mages closed on them slightly, and Rosher's hand went to his dagger.

Riena covered it, shaking her head. "Nay. This is my fight," she whispered.

Rosher looked to her in disbelief. She was depleted from channeling. Riena couldn't possibly use her magic effectively. She couldn't mean to fight them physically, either.

As if she read his thoughts, Riena patted his hand. "If you kill one of them, we will be caught. You know it is true."

He ground his teeth at that. She was right. There would be too many questions, if a Star Mage were killed, even one who was breaking laws, even if they were defending themselves. It was better to let her duel with them, though she would likely come away much the worse for it.

"The first opportunity that presents, you will go for help," he pleaded.

Riena met his gaze in the near total darkness, seeing more than he with eyes attuned to the night. "Yes." She cleared her throat, no doubt stalling for time, hoping that Zon and his brothers would come their way.

Rosher relaxed slightly, looking to the dark forms conferring a few body lengths away. If Riena made her escape, all was well. Worse even than her being injured was Riena being discovered for what she was and turned over to Etan and Karris.

He expected the Mages to stand aside or to attack outright. They did neither.

"We urge you to pay your time, Midman," the third man spoke up again.

"And if I still refuse?" she asked.

Rosher cried out as a branch whipped against his temple, drawing blood. Riena's hands flew out, and the branch retreated. More branches swayed toward them, then away, a dance of energy expended and rebuffed. It was a dance that Riena couldn't engage in for long.

He ducked another branch, looking from Mage to Mage desperately. He'd trained to protect her from non-magic attacks, not rogue Mages. What they were doing was illegal, punishable by hard labor or even death. But how could he and Riena possibly fight them? And what would be the punishment for dueling?

Riena threw her head back, and the branches above them parted, sending a shaft of moonlight to feed her fight. The Mages surged toward her, shouting their plans back and forth across the space between them, realizing the depth of her power abruptly. The branches they'd used turned on them, knocking the rogues to their backs.

"Run, Romik," Rosher thundered, turning to tackle the first Mage who found his feet. All she needed was a few moments to make it to help.

He tightened his hold on the Mage, wrestling with him as the other two gave chase. This one would face justice, even if the other two escaped it. "Still now, or I will break your neck," he growled.

The Mage fell silent and motionless beneath him, no doubt realizing that Rosher was more than capable of making that threat a reality.

It was several long moments before sounds returned. Rosher drew his dagger and placed it to the Mage's throat. If his fellows returned with Riena, this one would be the first to die.

"Companion Gerry?" a woman's voice called out, using the name he'd adopted when he and Riena fled. "Are you well?"

"I am," he replied.

"Then hand over the prisoner to me and return to your master."

Rosher looked up in surprise, grinding his teeth at the sight of the silver buttons glinting in the moonlight still shining through the hole Riena made in the branches. She was a royal bodyguard, and one misstep would see them caught—if they weren't already.

"Companion Gerry?"

He nodded, taking heart in her use of his assumed name. They were yet safe. Rosher pushed to his feet, sheathing his dagger and turning out of the forest at a full run.

He prayed that he'd not see star blue robes when he broke from the trees. Anything but star blue royal robes.

Chapter Six

"What is it?" Lena asked, her sword half-unsheathed with only his unease to drive her to action.

"Mages. More than one."

"A group channeling? There is a blight in these parts," she offered hopefully.

Karris shook his head, his feeling of unease growing as he examined the releases of power. It was choppy, not synchronized. "There is something wrong with the flow. As if— They seem to be working against each other."

Lena raised an eyebrow at that. "A duel?" Few Star Mages indulged in so stupid a pastime.

"Mayhap." He wished he could be certain.

His mount pranced, mirroring his mood. Karris guided him toward the stand of trees, following the feeling of discord.

"Karris," Lena hissed. "A duel is not your concern."

"Master Caiben," he reminded her, smoothing his black robes to punctuate the warning. "It is." As a Master, he would be expected to intervene. He would stand as judge and order punishment. It was his duty to do so.

She shook her head in disgust but took the lead to protect him as her training demanded of her.

A blast of power drowned out the smaller bursts, and Karris furrowed his brow in surprise. If it was a duel, what in the Mother's name was at stake?

"Run, Romik," a man bellowed.

Karris slid from his mount, soaking up the moon's fading light, preparing to aid a Mage in need.

A young Mage in the green robes of a Midman stumbled from the trees, looking to Karris in confusion. Then he was overtaken by two Mages in trousers and tunics, only the brown sashes they wore a sign of their status as Masons.

One grasped the young Mage by the back of his robes, pulling on the hood so that the material tore. The second laid a punch that dropped the young man to his knees, gasping for breath and pressing a hand to his injured ribs.

"Halt," Karris demanded, hoping that his command would be enough, that he wouldn't be forced to duel and possibly have to present himself to some judge for it.

The rogues turned to him, gaping at the sight of a Master Mage bearing witness to their crimes. They looked to the green-clad man in dismay. Their attention flicked to Lena, and their hands dropped to their sides.

Their reaction was to be expected. Even if they dared balk a Master Mage to hide their crimes, only one with a death wish balked a royal bodyguard protecting her charge. Nothing the rogues could do in this place would be fast enough to stop Lena from killing them with a well-aimed thrown blade.

Karris nodded, pulling his hood to shade his face, unwilling to give the rogues time to see through his disguise. "Are there more?" he asked.

"Gerry," the downed man managed, his eyes frantic.

"Another Mage?"

"Nay. My companion— With one of them."

Lena strode forward, motioning the rogues ahead of her. She wouldn't chance leaving them with Karris. It was in her training.

One look at the rogues told Karris that she had nothing to fear. They didn't intend to fight anyone now. They were resigned to their fates.

"I will end this," Lena growled, doubtless still peeved at being involved in this affair in the first place.

Karris nodded, stepping to the struggling Mage. He reached to help the man up, but Karris missed his mark as the Midman dodged his hands.

"I mean you no harm," Karris assured him. "Let me see to your injury and—"

The man dodged him again, fast though he was staggering and swaying with every movement. "Nay, Master. My companion..."

Karris stared at him in confusion. Why would his presence unnerve the young man? Karris settled on the ground, hoping to put him at ease. "What is your name, young Midman?" he asked in a soothing voice.

"Ro— Romik, Master." His breath still came in ragged movements of his narrow back. His dark hair cascaded half over his sweat-soaked face.

"Why did they attack you, Romik?"

"They are—" His chest seized, most likely in pain. "Former army men, Master."

Karris set his jaw, biting back a curse at that. There was no requirement for Mages to serve in the military. If there were, the uproar from the Great Mages would be deafening, to be sure. There were many honorable uses for power, and even wandering Mages for hire served a purpose that was indispensable.

"They will pay a heavy price," Karris promised. Lena would see to that immediately.

Romik raised his face slowly, seemingly uncertain for some reason. "My thanks, Master."

"May I see to your injuries now?" he offered, certain that the wall between them had been scaled.

Romik shook his head, his body trembling.

Karris had no time to question his strange reserve. A light-haired man bolted from the trees and knelt at Romik's side, heedless of the blood winding down his pale cheek and into his full beard. His gaze passed over Karris without interest or recognition.

Gerry eased Romik to his knees, his big hands testing his master's ribs. The young Mage's eyes closed, and he laid his head to his companion's shoulder. Gerry glanced at Karris as if gauging him for a response to the move, then looked away to his master again.

Karris winced. Were they lovers? Did Romik fear sanction under Mages' law for his inclinations? It was certainly possible. It would even explain the vehemence of the rogues' attack. If they knew—or even suspected Romik's possible tastes, they would use it as an excuse to be rough with the young man.

Romik rolled his forehead against Gerry's chest, and something stirred in Karris's memory, something uncertain. Romik looked over his shoulder, a glimmer of fear in his eyes as Lena left the forest with her prisoners in hand.

Karris gasped. The image was complete. He pushed to his feet, dragging a tent from his horse's cargo pouch.

Romik and his companion weren't lovers. They weren't what they seemed, at all. No wonder they feared him.

"Deliver them to the guards in town," he barked at Lena. *Before I run a blade through them, myself.* He calmed himself. Karris needed his wits about him for what was to come, and he needed time to calm himself before Lena read his fury. "I will see to our guests."

"Their punishment?" she asked formally.

He stilled, willing himself to reject the first penalty that came to mind, the one they'd earned. "Hard labor and thirty lashes," he ordered. "Each."

"As you wish," she answered.

The rogues paled, but they didn't protest the sentence he'd passed. They dared not, and if they dared that much, Karris would see them dead. He turned from them, making it clear that there would be no reconsidering their fate.

He set about unfolding the structure, while Rosher tended to Riena and Lena took the prisoners to their jailors. Yes, the rogues deserved death for abusing a woman, but ordering that would have told Lena more than Karris was ready to. There was too much to be lost by involving Lena at this point.

* * * *

Where is the royal bodyguard?" Riena whispered, exhaustion dragging her down.

"Gone to take the men to punishment."

She nodded. "We should be away then, before she returns."

Rosher flicked a glance at the Master Mage and nodded. He eased to his feet with Riena in his arms and turned to the trees. She tried not to consider what they were about to do.

There was no guarantee that Rosher would be able to collect their belongings before they ran. When the Master discovered them missing, he would know something was seriously wrong, and pursuit would come fast and hard. It was likely that they would run with only the wages they'd earned so far to see them through, making their way with her injured to avoid close inspection, losing as much as half of their amassed earnings to rebuild what was gone. Riena sighed at that.

"Halt, Gerry."

Rosher halted at the Master Mage's cry, a look of misery on his face.

"Use my tent to heal your young master," he continued.

Riena fisted her hand in Rosher's tunic. If they did that, the royal bodyguard would return before they were away, and there would be no chance of sneaking away. "We would not put you out of your shelter," she reasoned. "My injury is—"

"Untended," he snapped.

Riena closed her eyes, biting back tears at the sound of his approach. Rosher's heartbeat thundered against her ear. She opened her eyes, staring into the shadows of his black hood, shivering at the old wives' tales of the demon in black with no face who came for naughty children.

As if hearing her thoughts, the Mage pulled his hood back, baring his face to her. His eyes were full of concern that made her head swim. His hair was a mass of black curls that teased his collarbones around a lean face with high cheekbones and plump, dark lips. He was beautiful.

Riena blushed and looked away, lest he catch her staring and know her for what she was.

"My name is Caiben," he said more gently. "You will make use of my tent, and you will remain in my protection until I am satisfied that you are fully healed."

"It is not necessary," Riena began. *Fully healed?* Mother Moon, she would have to hide what she was for a month.

"Now, Midman Romik." His voice left no room for them to fight the command.

She nodded, and Rosher turned to the shelter, his muscles tense. He shouldered aside the flap and laid Riena on a sleeping pallet.

Riena inhaled Master Caiben's scent, biting her lower lip at the wave of heat it sent like tendrils of smoke through her stomach. She shook her head, nearly groaning as the movement released more of his musk from the bedding. Why did he affect her so markedly? Was his scent so different than Rosher's? Riena knew instinctively that it was.

"What now?" he whispered.

She winced, moving cautiously. "Tend to my wound. They do not know who we are, or the guard would have delivered us to judgment along with the rogues. We will take our leave as soon as I am able to walk unassisted. They cannot keep us longer than that."

"Unless they unmask us," he grumbled.

Riena shook her head, tears welling in her eyes at the reminder.

Rosher's eyes were pained, most probably at the sight of her tears. He kissed her forehead. "Pray your disguise holds."

She winced for a new reason.

* * * *

"Romik?" Karris called out, grinding his teeth at playing into this ridiculous farce.

The flap swung back, and Rosher bowed his head, waving Karris inside with the tray of food he carried.

"You can join Lena at the fire for your meal, Gerry," he offered cordially.

The big man looked up in surprise, his eyes narrowing. He let the flap slide shut behind Karris, then turned to kneel at Riena's side, playing the part of a faithful servant well. "I will see to myself, when my master sleeps."

"I will care for—him." Mother! It was maddening to know Riena for a woman and call her a man.

"Nay, Master Caiben. No one cares for Romik but myself." His voice was gruff, not quite a challenge, though it was close. A flash of pain lit in Riena's eyes, then was gone again, reminding Karris of her family position.

Even when Andren's companion had admitted the Great Mage's dalliance with Riena's mother at the appropriate time to have sired her, his family refused to consider that Riena might be of their line. Even when faced with the truth that only three houses in Voria were known for the ability to transfigure plants, they sneered at the idea that she might be Andren's child.

As for her mother's family— Better not to think about them. Their uncaring attitude always made Karris furious.

Karris nodded and set the tray next to Rosher, allowing the blond man to feed his battered sister. The tray was full of healing foods: roasted meat and bread, dried vegetables and even milk he'd had Lena purchase from a neighboring farmer. The fact that she'd likely woken the man to do so didn't bother Karris, for once.

"When I asked your name, you listed no family," Karris noted carefully.

Riena darkened. "I have none."

"What family were you then? Your father—"

"I never knew him," she interrupted him, talking around a bit of meat, "and my mother died when I was very young. Her name was Bentin."

Rosher's father's name. "How came you to have so loyal a companion?"

"Gerry was also without family. It is an equitable arrangement. He cares for me, and I provide for him." The story sounded practiced. Riena had obviously planned well for questioning.

"Why did I frighten you?" he pressed, testing her ability to fabricate.

"I had just been attacked—"

"Nay."

Rosher paused in offering Riena a bit of bread, his face tense.

"Nay," Karris repeated. "You feared *me*. Why did you?"

"His own master was barely tolerant," Rosher commented smoothly. "You can hardly blame Romik for his mistrust."

"Abusive?" Karris asked, stunned and amused at the same time. That was a mistake that could see her killed. Allegations of that sort—

"Impatient," Riena corrected him. "He rushed through my training and was rid of me."

Karris winced at the truth of that. From Riena's point of view, that was exactly what Master Jerin and the others would have done. "Have you sealed?" he asked, making no move to look for the sealing scars.

"Yes, Master."

He knew she had, of course, but Karris wanted to see if she would admit it without him forcing the issue. "Formidable for one as young as you are." He'd sealed at eighteen. The average age was twenty-two. Though Riena was nearly twenty, she looked younger than her age—perhaps seventeen now, indicating that she sealed at twelve or thirteen. That would be difficult to explain away under scrutiny.

Riena nodded silently, chewing a bit of meat.

"Considering your recent unpleasant encounter... Recite the three rules of travel, Romik."

She choked, blinking her eyes, seemingly in pain.

"Are you quite all right?"

"Yes, Master," she managed.

"The rules?" he reminded her, knowing full well that Riena couldn't answer the question, unless she'd stolen a copy of *The Master's Words*.

She looked to Rosher miserably. "I cannot," she admitted.

"Can you read?" he prodded.

"Of course, Master."

"But you cannot quote the simplest of rules from *The Master's Words*?"

Riena shook her head, struggling for words. "My master— He favored students who could line his pockets best. A poor penitent with no family, like myself, was worth only practical teaching."

A worthy lie. She might just have what it takes to survive this mad scheme after all. "And why did you not appeal to another master?"

Again she seemed to stumble over her words. "I believed..."

"Go on."

Riena lowered her gaze. "Are not all masters alike? I mean no offense," she hastened to add. "Already, you show yourself to be of different cloth than—"

Karris growled a curse, and Riena shied closer to Rosher. A plan took shape in his mind, a way to convince her to stay with him, when she clearly wished to escape him as quickly as possible.

"It seems we also can come to an equitable arrangement," he informed her.

Riena's brow furrowed. "In what way?"

"You require a teacher to complete your training."

She gasped in surprise at the offer. "And you?" Riena managed.

"A working team makes three times the coin. I will take two thirds and leave you your full share." Karris offered his hand. "Have we an arrangement?"

Riena seemed not to breathe. Her gaze flicked to Rosher, then away so as not to show weakness.

"Young Midman Romik?" he prodded her.

"May I consider it until next moonrise?" she asked formally.

Karris pulled his hand back, his heart heavy. "Of course." What would he do if she refused him? He hadn't wanted to resort to force.

* * * *

"Are you mad?" Rosher whispered fiercely.

Riena winced, and he immediately regretted his harsh tone. He squeezed her wrist gently in apology.

"I know his offer is tempting," Rosher continued. "I know you wish to finish your training."

"Think of the years to come, Rosher," she pleaded. "Some things are not difficult to hide. Lack of proper training is not one of them. As a Mason, I can earn so much more. You said so yourself before—"

"Later, when there is not so much a chance of being caught—"

"This chance may never come again."

She was right. *Mother take the winds of chance!* There was no denying that Riena was correct about that.

She was correct about so many things. If Master Caiben raised her to Mason—again, she could earn a quarter times more for her work than she did now. This chance would likely never come again, and Riena would be consigned to acting the part of a Midman forever, with no hope of improvement, if she refused it now.

He sighed, nodding his approval.

Riena pressed a hand to her cracked rib, grimacing.

"More willow bark?" he offered.

"No. I—" She sighed.

"What is it?"

"I will be making him a traitor," she whispered, miserable again.

"Unknowing. Etan could not possibly—"

"Could he not? Are you certain of that?" she asked. "I admit that I am not."

Rosher hesitated. Etan was a hard man when crossed. No one argued that point.

"I thought not."

He stroked her chin. "What will you do?"

Riena took a deep breath, as deep as her sore ribs allowed. "I will plead for his life if it comes to that. This chance will never come again."

* * * *

Caiben stilled, panning his gaze over the blue robes tossed negligently over Karris's throne, cursing fluently at what it might signify. "What has he done this time?" he asked, knowing Etan would be fuming in some close corner, waiting for Caiben to ask.

"Disappeared," Etan grumbled.

Caiben chuckled at that. Karris was no end of amusement.

"You find that humorous? My son left behind the trappings of a prince at Riena's home, left no indication of what he intends, and vanished into a misty morn. What is so amusing, Master Caiben?"

"Mayhap that you so easily forget your own youth," he chided his king in a manner honed over almost four decades of practice. "I remember King Evard sending more than a few companies of guards and soldiers after you in your day." *Before you took Sabina as your mate and retired your restless ways.*

It wouldn't do to remind Etan of that, he cautioned himself. It would only send his king further into melancholy. Though he'd never convinced Sabina to soulbind with him, Etan fancied a memory of her as the perfect wife—his only love, though Caiben had tried to tell him about Sabina's wandering eye more than once.

It was no surprise to Caiben that Sabina would not soulbind. If Etan had felt her true emotions through the link it would forge, her days in pampered luxury would end, even if it killed Etan to achieve it. Such a thing *would* have killed him, once they had soulbound.

Etan had always been more devoted to Sabina than Sabina had been to him and to Karris. Luckily, Karris was undeniably Etan's son. If he were not, Caiben would have had to take the problem head on. As it was, there was little danger in Etan's fantasy of his dead wife. How could there be?

Etan stepped before him, his youthful face harsh as any bandit's. "After *us*, Caiben."

"I recall Evard commenting that he wished they'd lose me to some accident, on more than one occasion." Strange as it seemed, Evard always believed Caiben was responsible for Etan's mad forays from princely duties. The former king never appreciated that his son lived on many an occasion only by the grace of Caiben's skill and pure luck. Caiben sighed. Mayhap Evard's certainty stemmed from how the pair met.

"Were we right?" Etan asked, seemingly driving at some point that eluded Caiben.

Caiben furrowed his brow. "Etan?"

"Was my father wrong to have us tracked down and dragged back?"

"Of course not." If Evard had been more intelligent, he would have shackled his son with something better than a scheming wife.

Etan stroked his chin. "I am happy to hear you admit it." He turned away, ambling across the throne room.

"Why should I not admit that? We were young and foolish." *Unmated. Without a care to duty.*

"Admitting it indicates your willingness to be charged with the deed."

Caiben's stomach lurched at that. "Deed, Etan? What deed?"

"Bring him back, Caiben."

"Me? But why do you not—"

Etan waved off his half spoken suggestion. "Nay. On the remote chance that Karris is doing as I ordered in some...mad fashion, I cannot send a company after him."

"And if he is doing as you ordered? Should I return with word and warn him to keep you apprised of his whereabouts?"

Etan looked to the setting moon. "Return him to me. I should have taken on the problem of Riena personally to begin with."

Caiben winced at that. Karris's faults aside, Caiben had no doubts that Riena was safer with Karris than with Etan. "Why me?"

"You know him, Caiben. You doubtless know Karris better than I do. He has never forgiven me." Etan fisted his hand loosely.

"I know." In this, Caiben knew Karris better than Etan did. For years, he had listened to Karris rant over the laws his father had broken. The prince had long ago surrendered any feelings of respect for the man who'd sired him.

Etan, as with all things, saw only what he wished to see. He saw a spoiled prince who balked at having his bride chosen for him. Caiben knew Karris's true concerns, his mistrust of a king who so easily sacrificed the law to his own avarice.

Caiben saw the strength and purity of the king Karris would one day be, something Etan feared most of all. Caiben knew he feared it, because it was something Etan would never acknowledge, something he denied vehemently.

"Will you go, Caiben? Or should I find someone else?"

"I will, but finding Karris will not prove an easy task."

"You know where young men go," Etan dismissed the warning.

Caiben nodded. Again, Etan saw what he wished. It was true that Caiben knew where young men like Etan would go. But Karris was nothing like his father. The question was where Karris would go.

Chapter Seven

Mey 6th, 4015

Lena watched, as Gerry guided his master to the fireside. The blond man was tense and formal. He'd not met her gaze since that moment in the trees the night before. It was to be expected. Many men feared the fierce women of the royal guard. He met her eyes briefly, his deep blue catching her attention, as turbulent as the eastern sea. Nay. This man didn't fear her, though his expression made her wonder what he did feel.

Gerry intrigued her.

She'd been incensed at Karris's decision to offer instruction to Midman Romik. His explanation that it was his duty to right a grievous wrong did little to mollify her. His further assertion that the young Mage's presence would make them less conspicuous had earned only her grudging consent.

Lena ranged her eyes over Gerry again. If Romik's companion was half the diversion he seemed able to be, Karris could indulge his overactive sense of duty until his "intended" fled Voria for good. There were worse things that could happen to her cousin than being rid of that snake, at any rate. Mayhap allowing Karris to forget his duty to find Riena would be a good thing.

"Have you come to a decision, Romik?" Karris asked.

The young Mage sipped a mug of water, not meeting Karris's earnest gaze. "I believe we have much to offer each other, Master Caiben. I am a diligent worker. In exchange for your teaching, your purse will support you well."

Lena bit back a snort of laughter at that. As if Karris needed the coin they'd earn! Mayhap he intended to give it to some charitable cause—or even to the young Midman, when they parted company.

Karris nodded, the tension easing from his shoulders. "A wise decision. If Gerry would see clear to leave you in my hands, your instruction will begin."

Gerry waited for his master's nod, then rose, smoothing his tunic. "I will collect our belongings and the food we are owed," he offered gruffly, turning away.

Lena followed him, anxious to make her purpose clear to him. It took Gerry only a few moments to realize she was trailing him, much faster than most men would have.

He glanced her way, stiffening, mayhap a bit wary. "You wish to speak to me, Guard Lena?"

She matched his stride. "It seems we will be traveling together."

"It does," he replied simply.

"You do not approve of that," she noted. *Mayhap we have more in common than the companions we keep.*

Gerry shrugged his broad shoulders. "Romik's choices are his own. It is not my place to approve. It is my place to serve."

She smiled at that, at the idea of Gerry serving her for a time. "How long have you served your master?"

He smiled a radiant smile that nearly stopped her heart. "Sometimes, it seems forever."

"Romik is a difficult master?" she asked in surprise. The Midman had seemed aloof but not harsh to her.

"Nay. A most fair and caring master. It is simply the life that is sometimes unkind...as you saw last night."

Lena sobered at that. "You did well, as well as could be expected against three rogue Mason Mages."

Gerry's jaw tightened. He nodded once, decisively.

"Your master was fatigued and still—"

He shot her a quelling look. Lena gasped in surprise at the strength of this man, falling a few steps behind as he drew near the farmer's home and disappeared inside to collect the things he came for.

She waited for him, wondering at Gerry's reaction. Romik had been overworked and outmatched. There was nothing shameful in that.

He reappeared, a pack on each shoulder and a huge bag of food grasped in one big hand. Gerry strode past her as if intent on ignoring her presence. Lena followed with a grumble of frustration.

"Is there a problem, Guard Lena?"

She matched his stride again. "Must we be adversaries?" she asked.

Gerry stopped, turning to her, his eyes searching out hers in the dim light. "Was I being adversarial?" he answered a little too innocently.

"My apologies, Guard Lena. It would seem I am unpracticed in the niceties of society."

"Then we can enjoy each other's company?" she asked.

His brow furrowed. "In what way?"

Lena resisted the urge to roll her eyes. Would she have to lead him through by his male parts? She trailed her fingertips down his stomach suggestively.

Gerry's breath hissed out, his face showing signs of stark male interest. She smiled at that. Was that why he didn't look at her? Did he believe she had no interest in him? Lena trailed her fingers lower, her body responding as he stiffened beneath her fingers.

Gerry stilled her hand. "I am not a youth to be toyed with, Guard Lena," he growled.

"You do not wish to lay with me?" she asked, daring him to deny the evidence that she held cradled in her hand.

"I do not perform to any woman's whims."

"And you believe I wish that?" she asked.

"Do you not?"

"Nay. I—"

He pushed her hand away, continuing on toward their camp.

Lena shouldered around him and stepped in Gerry's path, confusion warring with her anger. "I do not treat men as bought servants," she informed him.

Gerry ranged his gaze down her body, and her nipples hardened against her uniform. Lena crossed her arms over them, annoyed with her response when she intended to discuss this with him.

He laughed harshly at that. "As I thought."

"You thought what?" she demanded.

"I have met your kind before."

"How dare you—"

"Women like you want to remain in control. Tell a man how to please them—what they *admit* pleases them instead of trusting him to listen to their bodies sing."

Lena stared at him in disbelief. Did he think her an unschooled maid? She'd taken men for the last five years and rarely left unsatisfied from the encounters. "I have *never*—"

The packs he carried hit the ground, and his hands closed on her hips. Gerry's mouth covered hers, seeking, caressing.

She groaned. This was what she wanted...nearly. A bit more intense—

Gerry pulled away with a shake of his head. "You see? You enjoyed my kiss and still you demanded something different."

"There is something wrong with seeking what feels best?"

"Does it?"

"Does—"

Gerry cupped her cheeks, his mouth brushing over hers, firing her arousal. He parted her lips, giving her just a taste of him before he pulled back.

"Does it?" he asked in a voice that spoke his restraint clearly.

Lena shook her head slowly, her mind spinning, trying to piece together what he'd just done to her, how he had made her ache with so simple a kiss.

He nodded, taking a step back, retrieving his packs. Gerry met her gaze, then brushed past her again.

"Gerry?" she called.

"Yes, Guard Lena?"

"I do not understand."

Gerry turned to her, smiling. His fingertips caressed her lips. "Consider this. Consider what you have learned this night."

"I want—"

His smile disappeared. Gerry sighed, turning away.

"What did I—"

"Consider it." His voice was edged in annoyance. Then Gerry was gone.

Lena stared after him, her body in a riot for him. Her lips tingled from his kiss, her hands shook, and her womb was heavy and aching. She growled a curse at his departing form.

* * * *

Riena watched Caiben from beneath her lashes, finishing the roast meat, bread, and broth as quickly as she could. The last thing she wanted was to keep the master waiting.

He didn't move. He didn't question her further. Caiben seemed content to study her silently, and that unnerved Riena most of all. Not knowing his mind made her itch to run from him.

She set her bowl down, forcing her hands not to shake. "I thank you for your kindness, Master Caiben."

"You are my student, Romik. I am responsible for your care and safety."

Riena darkened in embarrassment. She'd spent the last decade actively avoiding being indebted to anyone but Etan, and she'd run from that entanglement. It was difficult to accept that someone besides Rosher felt that kind of bond with her again.

His next words stole her breath. "And still you fear me. What reason have I given you to fear me?"

"I—" She fumbled for words. As always, Riena seemed to lose her composure around Caiben. In a month of running, no man had scattered her this way.

No man has had the opportunity to question me so closely, her mind argued. Riena grasped at that. That was the reason he unnerved her. That and the fact that he traveled with a royal bodyguard.

She forced her mind back to his question. Her real reasons for fearing him would see her delivered to Etan and Karris, she was certain. What else was there? "I have not known a fond reception from our brother Mages in my life," she stammered.

It wasn't entirely untrue. Masters Jerin and Korl had been stiff and formal with her. Whether that was because of the King's Right, having to change their styles of teaching to accommodate not letting her know the laws that led them, that they weren't comfortable with a female Mage, or because they didn't care for her company personally, she didn't know. Even Etan had hated her on sight. Karris hated her still.

Caiben nodded. "I am not the jealous type. Nor do I care only for how well one can line my pockets."

She nodded, glad that he hadn't questioned her further about her dealings with Star Mages. In truth, Riena had dealt with few. She avoided them when she could now, but no Mage who hadn't been ordered to do so went out of his way to interact with her before she ran. There was little to tell.

"I would appreciate it if you would call me Caiben. Master will prove acceptable in the company of night-sleepers and strange Mages. Am I understood Romik?"

"Yes, Ma— Yes, Caiben."

"Excellent. Now, I would like to test your abilities. I realize you are depleted from the duel last night, but I will glean much from even a small outlay of power."

Riena furrowed her brow. "But, I am trained in practical—" She swallowed hard at his raised eyebrow. "As you wish, Master."

He sighed at that.

"Caiben," she corrected herself quickly. She cursed herself. Why, when she'd ached for years that others kept her at arm's length, did a single Mage who invited her friendship make her uneasy?

Because it is dangerous to become close to this man. Dangerous to her freedom and dangerous to her piece of mind.

Riena looked around the clearing, hoping not to meet his eyes. "What should I do?"

Caiben pushed to his feet and offered her his hand. Riena pretended not to notice and got to her feet with a swallowed groan. He nodded and led her to a stand of trees with Pink Daughters growing on young bushes around the trunk.

"The trees?" she asked, looking automatically for signs of shade rot or oak bend and seeing none.

"No. The flowers. The trees block much of their light."

Riena looked up at the thick branches, nodding. "Yes. I see it clearly."

"Help them grow, Romik."

She bit back a gasp as Caiben pressed his chest to her back. His hands cradled hers as Etan once had. Even Master Jerin had never held her this intimately. Her heart stuttered as it surely had when Etan touched her, but this time her disquiet was for a new reason.

Touch was either a pleasure or agony. The touch of a teacher was always a pleasure, but all of her former teachers had been men far her senior. Caiben was different. He was young, beautiful, and distracting to her on a very sexual level. Riena ground her teeth at the truth of that, trying desperately to reason her way out of her arousal. The sensation of a young man touching her in an intimate manner was new.

She bit her lip. Had *any* man younger than Rosher ever touched her? Well, there was Karris, but he hadn't touched her kindly. Riena sobered.

No one young had ever touched her kindly. Not in her lifetime.

The village children had never played with her. If her grandfather's displeasure hadn't discouraged them, their parents' wary attitudes did. After Etan claimed her for Karris in King's Right, no man but her teachers, Etan, and Rosher had dared touch her. Since she'd run, Rosher had prevented any man from laying hands on her socially for fear they would feel her bound breasts or detect the slight difference in her personal musk that marked her as a female Mage instead of male.

Yes. Caiben was the first—

"Romik?" Caiben's voice was unreadable. Was he concerned for her or angry at her inattention? "If you are too worn—"

"Nay, Master. My apologies."

Riena concentrated on her task, sick at the idea of angering Caiben when she needed him so desperately.

I need his teaching, she corrected herself.

She laid her head back, forcing herself not to startle as she nestled into the hollow of Caiben's shoulder, soaking in the moon's radiance, feeling the shiver of power bloom into a roaring torrent. Riena kept strict control, easing the magic into the flower bushes and helping them grow.

Caiben's breathing became ragged. His breath teased at her forehead, swirling the second skin of energy surrounding her. It was always like this when a teacher tested or guided her, sharing in her release of power.

He shifted, pressing his body closer. The heavy length of his member nestled tight to her lower back, and the buzz of arousal in her exploded into a soul-deep ache the likes of which only a rebirth typically brought. Riena sucked in her breath, but the centering she hoped for slipped her grasp with the lungful of Caiben's musk she took in.

"Yes, Romik. Excellent."

His voice caressed her face, making Riena all too aware of how close he was, how easy it would be for his lips to find hers. She sobered, shaking herself mentally. He thinks I am a man. He *must* think that, or Rosher and I will be delivered to justice.

Riena forced her mind back to her task, changing her focus and purpose.

Caiben startled at the groaning of the great oak above them, his face leaving hers as he looked up. "What are you doing?" he demanded.

She didn't answer. Riena needed every drop of concentration on her task.

The pulse of sexual pleasure beat hard in her womb. She pressed back into Caiben as the waves of delight took her, the flow of power lost with her shattered discipline.

Riena stumbled, her knees buckling. Caiben caught her against him, and she gasped at the length of his forearm wrapped around her bound breasts. If the Mother was kind, he would believe them part of the binding over her injured ribs. Caiben lowered her to the ground, still wrapped in his arms, his face buried in her hair and his breath hot on her skin.

"Why did you reform the tree?" He didn't sound angry. He seemed genuinely confused by her actions.

She closed her eyes, fumbling for words in her muddled mind. "The growth I fed the Pink Daughters is fleeting. The trees steal their light, night after night."

He laughed, a sound of pure joy. "Such incredible foresight," Caiben mused. "By encouraging the tree to grow aside, you guaranteed the flowers a share of the moon's light in years to come."

"It— It seemed the best way to accomplish the task you set."

"Indeed it was. Better than I had considered. You are strong, Midman Romik. Tell me. Why is it that you wear green when your power places you as a high Mason or even a Master?"

She didn't have to consider that question. "I have power, Caiben, but I lack knowledge of *The Master's Words*. As such, I cannot claim a higher rank."

Caiben sighed, his body still wrapped around hers. "The knowledge you will have," he vowed. "I will have you in Master's black, before you leave me."

Chapter Eight

Riena stiffened in his arms, and Karris shivered as his lips brushed her neck. Her skin still radiated the energy she'd channeled, and her scent taunted him. Holding Riena in the aftermath of her sexual climax, his body pressed to hers, was sublime, but it did nothing to ease his state of arousal.

"The rank of Mason would suit me," she managed in a strained voice. "I seek no more for myself."

Karris forced his eyes open, blushing as understanding crashed over him. Riena couldn't claim the rank of Master. Masters were charged by the throne, named by Etan in test, when the Master recommending them sent them on. She could never present herself to Etan, and so she could never stay with a Master long enough to be sent on.

"As you wish," he answered evenly.

Riena moved to push herself from Karris's embrace. He released her, a numb acknowledgement of her need to escape his touch before he discovered her secret.

"Are you fatigued?" Karris asked calmly, grinding his teeth at the loss of her warmth.

"No. I just..."

"Go to the fire, Romik. I will collect *The Master's Words* from my pack." He thanked the Mother silently that he'd brought a copy along to complete his disguise.

Riena was at the fireside when he returned. She didn't meet his gaze when he handed the book to her. Riena seemed barely to breathe. Her fingers traced the design etched into the cover reverently, and she bowed her head as if in a mute prayer of thanks before a feast.

"Have you ever held a copy of the great book before?" Karris asked carefully.

"No." She fingered the edge, as if she were afraid to open it and see what had been stolen from her.

He grimaced. Had her teachers kept the book under lock? It was likely.

If she read it, Riena would know the laws his father had broken. She could appeal to another kingdom—or to the Great houses. Either would gladly aid her against Etan, if she knew to ask. If it wouldn't have been decreed an act of treason against his father, Karris would have told her himself, years ago.

"Open the book, Romik. Begin with the history of the Star Mages. You will know all before you leave me."

And she *would* leave him if Karris didn't convince her to him. That thought was painful. Where he would have done anything to free her only days ago, now that Karris knew her, he found walking away much more difficult. Would she appeal for help in leaving him? If she did, he had to release her, though he would do anything to hold her close.

But how to convince her and not reveal what he knew of her? That was the true difficulty.

* * * *

Rosher spent the time Caiben worked with Riena storing their possessions in the tent they'd used the night before and handing off the pallet Riena had used to Guard Lena. He glanced at her often, feigning indifference when the bodyguard caught him watching and turned away in red-faced embarrassment, her back stiff and regimental.

In truth, Rosher was more affected by Guard Lena than he wanted to admit. It had seemed like a good idea at the time, playing on the bodyguard's interest to keep her focus on himself instead of Riena. Of course, he had tried to dissuade her first, playing coy games and acting the obtuse, uneducated fool for her to make it seem more trouble than prudent to pursue him.

When his aim had changed from playing with her to earnest interest was an uncertain thing. At some point as he kissed her, he lost track of his plan to make her wait—to ensure Guard Lena wouldn't become bored and start looking for something new and available of interest to her.

A royal bodyguard's fixed attraction to Riena would spell their doom. Riena was hardly prepared to rebuff such a deadly game.

Rosher glanced to Guard Lena again out of the corner of his eye. By the Mother, how could an enemy be so sexually appealing? It wasn't simply abstinence talking for him. There was something about this guard that made Rosher ache to have her in his bed—but not on her terms. *Never* on her terms. He'd met too many royal bodyguards like her to accept that frustration again.

Master Jerin's royal-trained guard seemed to view Rosher much as she would a bed servant. Guard Dera had played at Rosher's need and inexperience, coming to his bed one day as Riena slept down the hall and making him feel there was something meaningful in her play. She'd used him to find what she wanted and tossed him aside when she tired of him—all to quickly for his tastes.

Other guards had tried the same. Rosher theorized that he was simply so different than the Mages they spent their nights with that they viewed him as a novelty, a golden toy.

Rosher hadn't played the game quite to their rules since Guard Dera. For a time, he'd played out their urges for a single encounter, then refused them more, silently laughing at their frustrated attempts to lure him back to bed with them. When the guards came to see this as a new and challenging sport, his tactics had changed.

Brushing off a royal bodyguard and latching onto the first willing maid in defiant show had been more enjoyable for Rosher. The maids were more than happy to play the game Rosher's way, and their satisfied smiles always infuriated the bodyguards who hoped to bed him.

Even that had grown tiresome. In some way, mayhap by allowing a guard to determine when he would actively seek release, Rosher was still playing their game, even as he balked them.

Guard Lena would be different. This time, it was Rosher's game. Whether she sought a man elsewhere or gave Rosher precisely what he wanted, he would emerge the winner. Of course, Guard Lena was stubborn. He and Riena might well part company with Master Caiben and Guard Lena, before she exercised either of those options.

* * * *

Riena closed the tent flap, sinking to Rosher's chest in exhaustion, her head spinning, full of pages of new information.

It wasn't simply the learning, she reminded herself. Caiben had all but created a new order in her life. The things Rosher had begged her to see to for weeks were now agreed upon. Caiben had insisted that she needed a tent to escape the sun in peace and horses to reach farms quicker and to speed travel in poor weather.

Though she agreed that he was right, she drew the line at charity. Riena had insisted that she pay him a fair price for this tent, though he argued its age and wear. He was lying, though she dared not accuse him of such openly.

Her brother shifted, and a waft of familiar scent assaulted her senses. Riena recoiled, pushing Rosher away with a growl of disgust.

He darkened. "It is not what you think," he whispered.

"You tumbled her," she stated miserably. How could Rosher be so careless and unthinking? "What happens when—"

"I did not. Our circling will buy time for you to learn from Master Caiben. As long as Guard Lena is intent on me, she will not have time to spare for you."

Riena bit back a sob. Rosher hated playing the sex games of the royal bodyguards. "I—I should leave. I cannot ask this of you."

Rosher chuckled, a purely male sound of amusement that she had never been able to recreate, despite hours of trying.

"Actually, playing bait to Guard Lena is the most enjoyable part of this whole mad expedition." He sobered. "And you cannot let this opportunity pass you by."

She threw her arms around his chest. "If you become uncomfortable, we will take our leave," she vowed.

He buried his face in her shoulder, inhaling her scent slowly. His fingers tightened on her hips. "Romik," he grumbled in the voice he'd used when she was a child misbehaving.

Riena darkened in understanding. "It is not what you think," she assured him, wincing that she was certainly lying. It was very much what he thought. Riena prayed that Rosher wasn't lying as well.

"You climaxed," he stated calmly. "I know the smell of it."

He should, she fumed. Rosher had taken enough women to bed to be a master at detecting a woman's state of arousal or release. "You know the channeling is—"

"You have never lost control this way before." His voice was a strained whisper, too knowing for Riena's peace of mind.

"I have never had a teacher as..." *Sexy. Young. Arousing. Beautiful.*

"Yes?" he prodded, his gaze shooting to the tent flap as if he meant to pummel Caiben for daring so much as touching her.

"Powerful as Caiben." She hadn't lied about that.

"Caiben?" Rosher growled. "He asks you—"

"He prefers that I call him by his given name in private," she whispered desperately. "Please...Gerry."

He nodded, taking the hint that he couldn't approach Caiben on such a matter while they were hiding what they were. "You know the risks. When... If you become uncomfortable—"

"I know." She did know, and Riena could never allow it to come to that. This chance was too important to sacrifice to carnal urges, no matter how powerful those needs were.

* * * *

Karris looked at Lena in surprise. His cousin lay on her pallet, seemingly furious.

"What is it?" he asked. Whatever it was, Karris had to settle it quickly. Lena in a foul mood would be disastrous to the stable environment he needed to cultivate. Riena was ready to bolt at any moment, and an unstable royal bodyguard would send her running again.

"He refused me," she fumed.

"R— Gerry?" He winced at how close he'd come to calling the man by his true name.

"Of course, Gerry." She managed a vicious smile. "It would be sweet revenge if I took his young master to—"

"Nay," Karris demanded, his heart pounding.

Lena looked to him in surprise. "You have never interfered in my sexual exploits before. Why now?"

"I need Romik, and I have a duty to right the wrongs done him. I cannot allow another."

She scowled. "I would just—"

"Play with him," Karris spat, suddenly disgusted at the idea.

Lena gaped at him.

"What is it?"

"He said the same of me," she noted miserably. "Do I really—"

Karris didn't hesitate. "Yes. You do."

Lena bit at her lip.

He nodded. If anyone would recognize her games, Rosher would. It was rumored that he had redefined the game. "Do you intend to keep playing?" he asked simply.

She didn't seem to know the answer to that.

"If Gerry knows your game," he prodded her, leaving the end hanging for her to follow the flow of logic. *And he does. He knows it very well.*

"He will not play." Her distraction said it all. Lena didn't know how *not* to play.

Karris sighed at the sudden preoccupation Lena fell into. Already, she was planning her next move. Already, she was forging on to her own doom. He stretched out on his pallet, resigned. If Lena meant to continue on a course that would not yield what she sought, it was not his concern.

As long as Lena played her games on Rosher instead of Riena, Karris didn't care what games she chose to play.

He sighed again, curling onto his pallet then stilling in surprise. Damn! He'd forgotten that Riena had used his pallet all day. Considering his tenuous control when she climaxed in his arms, her scent was likely to drive him mad. *What a way to be driven mad!* Karris breathed in the scent he'd missed for so long.

Chapter Nine

Mey 8th, 4015

Lena smiled. It was about time! She'd started to fear that Gerry would never show up, though he typically came down to the water at this time of night on various errands, from collecting water to gathering herbs for his master's comfort.

He was quiet about his watching. Lena had to give the man that much praise, though she would make him beg for more than that.

She made a show of her bathing, cupping her breasts, running her hands down the flat plane of her stomach, throwing her short hair back. Still, minutes passed without a sound from Gerry—of his breathing or clothing landing on the ground, of a protest nor even of him walking away. He didn't join her.

Lena turned her head toward the shore as if it were a negligent move, with no more purpose than squeezing water from her hair...and the clapping started. She stared at him in a mixture of fury and stunned fascination.

Gerry stood on the shore, his stance careless, one shoulder snug to a willow trunk, clapping with a mocking smile on his rugged face. "You must have studied with a master thespian," he called out, "or perhaps a consort trainer."

She fumbled for words, finally settling on a growl that held the promise of his slow and painful death.

"Well, go on then." He motioned carelessly, as if Lena would perform for him.

Well, wasn't I doing just that a moment ago? She fisted her hands at the truth of that.

Gerry chuckled at her irritation. "I thought, since you were enjoying yourself so much, you might want to continue."

She hadn't been. Not really. Knowing Gerry was watching had given her a thrill but only as long as Lena believed she was driving him mad with the sight of her play.

"Guard Lena?"

She glared at him. Lena was fast beginning to loathe the sound of that name on his lips.

"If that is what you want, why do you not continue, Guard Lena?" Gerry cocked an eyebrow at that, ranging his gaze over her as if gauging a horse or bull at market.

Lena snapped. She splashed water at him, noting the drops that stained the suede of his boots a shade darker in grim satisfaction. "It is not what I *want*," she thundered.

"Oh?" He stroked a hand over his golden beard. "Is it not?"

"Nay! Mother take you! You know it is not, you—you insufferable male."

"Then why do you do it?"

She fought for words again, cursing her inability to think clearly around Gerry. Why couldn't he simply act like any other male and be done with this insanity?

Gerry squatted on the grass, shaking his head. "You played this act for me?"

As if he doesn't know that I did! She crossed her arms over her chest, feeling inexplicably chastised as she hadn't since shortly after she'd started her training as a royal bodyguard.

"Ah, lovely Guard Lena," he murmured. "Why would you try this? Why, when I told you I would not dance to your pipe?"

She shook her head.

"Do we understand each other now?" he prodded her.

"Yes."

His smile disappeared. "You are a beautiful woman, Guard Lena. Though your—theatrics had not the intended result on me, I will admit that it had *some* effect."

Her breath caught at that. "Will you—"

Gerry stood abruptly. "Nay. I believe we have exhausted my patience this moonset. Sleep well, Guard Lena." He strode away, leaving her aching for him for a second time, something no man had managed in her life.

* * * *

Rosher growled a curse on the woman, pleading with the Mother to ease his ache for her. He fumed that Guard Lena had played at his arousal this way. He'd warned her, and if Rosher dared ask Riena to turn her back on her training, Guard Lena would see his back.

Would she? Some dark corner of his mind taunted Rosher with visions of Guard Lena's performance for him. Had any royal bodyguard gone so far to tempt him? Had he ever been so tempted by anything they did?

Never. His body ached for her. It had since the first time she'd touched herself. "Guard Lena," he growled.

She'd nearly broken him. Acting unaffected while she all but begged him to ride on her like a bull in rutt had pushed Rosher to his limits. Keeping the arousal from his voice, laughing, and clapping gaily for her had taken every drop of his will.

Rosher halted. He wanted her, and he wasn't afraid to admit it, but this discomfort would be returned to her in full measure. Rosher smiled. Before he finished with her, Guard Lena would regret this night. He'd meant her to hear his approach tonight. The next time, he would come by stealth.

* * * *

Mey 11th, 4015

Rosher ran his fingers down the line of Guard Lena's ribs, grasping her weapon hand as she turned on him. Her eyes opened wide in surprise. She looked to his hand, rigid and stunned by the success of both his approach and his attack.

"You see," he soothed her. "Did I have to ask what you wanted? My touch was unwelcome."

Uncertainty filled her eyes. Her muscles relaxed beneath his hands. "So quiet," she mused.

Rosher raised an eyebrow at that, hiding his irritation at her behind a bored look. He was in command, and he would not lose that place to a useless fit of temper. He'd encountered that surprise from royal bodyguards before, and though it was an insult to him, it was a predictable and useful reaction of the cockiest of the guards.

"You believe only females are capable of stealth and speed." *Most royal bodyguards do.* "I assure you that Romik chose well when he chose me as his companion." The truth of that statement and the fear inherent in balking King's Right were the only reasons Etan had agreed not to assign a noble-born guard to Riena long ago.

"I did not," she began in something resembling an apology.

He gleaned an opportunity to play out the game a little longer. This discussion had always been a source of frustration for him, and he'd never had the ability to fully turn the tables on a royal bodyguard before.

"The only reasons royal guards have traditionally been female are because the fragile Star Mages found them less threatening than males, and they were often daughters or granddaughters of other powerful Mages, which made them somewhat—advantageous in other respects."

Guard Lena blanched. "You dare—"

"Call Romik fragile? He is in many ways. Ask him. He does not deny it. The weak morning sun burns his pale skin. He will never be as strong as I am, though he is unarguably fast. He is weakened by his channeling, on the verge of collapse when the healing is intense. Is it not so with Master Caiben?"

"I did not—"

"Or perhaps you are offended by my certainty that the most powerful Star Mages have taken lovers or mates from Great Mage lineage to strengthen bloodlines."

She darkened, her mouth opening as if to issue a protest.

"Deny it, then. Tell me you are more than three generations removed from three Great or Royal households."

Guard Lena gaped at him, seemingly at a loss for words.

Rosher laughed at that. "You cannot do it. Which families can you claim within three generations?"

She pulled her wrist from his grasp, pushing past Rosher and storming off toward the camp, her arms crossed over her chest.

He matched her, enjoying seeing her so out of control. "The closest one then. What Great house most closely claims you? Or is it the Royal house that—"

"It is not the Royal house," she snapped.

"Then which?"

Guard Lena turned on him, beautiful in the pure force of her anger. It was probably the most honest emotion he'd seen from her yet. This wasn't posturing and bruised pride. This was fury, an emotion he'd wager she seldom indulged in.

"My grandfather was Great Mage Andren."

Rosher's stomach turned to ice at that. Guard Lena was a much more dangerous foe than he'd realized. If she learned who Riena was, she'd stop at nothing to see his sister dead or in Karris's bed.

Guard Lena's face erupted in a wide smile. "I see you know the name," she taunted.

"Yes. I do. That places you with at least three Great houses and the Royal line within the last four generations, if memory serves." He shrugged, adopting a disinterested look again. "More inbred than most, but not unexpected given your— temperament."

She slapped his face.

Rosher had her hand captured in his before she could withdraw. He met her startled look, kissing her palm. "I trust you have no interest in sex with me," he guessed.

Guard Lena's expression was abruptly uncertain. She stumbled over the beginnings of an answer.

He nodded and turned away. "Let me know your choice when I come to you next."

Rosher didn't wait for her to hurl insults or rocks at his retreating back. He made his way back to the light-blocking tent they'd purchased from Caiben, formulating a plan to keep Guard Lena focused on himself.

* * * *

"Mother take that man," Lena cursed, smoothing her pallet with what amounted to well-laid punches.

Karris bit back a laugh. Though Lena didn't know it, she was playing the game with a grand master. Rosher had stymied nearly every royal bodyguard he'd encountered in the last decade.

"What has Gerry done now?" he asked innocently, feigning interest in the great book.

Two more punches laid the stuffing as flat as she no doubt wanted to land her opponent.

Karris raised the book to hide the smirk on his face. "Lena?" he called sweetly.

"He said— That pompous, arrogant—"

Laughter tickled at his throat, and Karris swallowed it down. "He certainly made an impression."

She glared at him. "When this is over with, I want your permission to kill him."

Karris sobered at that. "What could he possibly say to—"

"Inbred," she growled.

"Pardon?" Surely, Lena hadn't just dared call Karris—

"He called *me* inbred."

He laughed heartily at that, picturing her reaction to the insult. Lena, like most of her line, took her affiliations seriously. She wore them with pride. Of course, her closest affiliations would be a source of annoyance to Rosher for the heartache they'd caused Riena over the years.

"You find this funny?" she demanded.

"He does have a point."

"What?" Lena came to her feet, her hand gripping the hilt of her dagger.

Karris raised an eyebrow at that. She darkened, glancing to her hand and easing it away with a stricken look.

He nodded. "We are a rather heavily cross-bred group, you know."

"Kar—"

He glared at her in warning.

"Caiben," she ground out from between clenched teeth. "What are you saying?"

"I am stating that new blood might be best."

"Like your *intended*?" she asked, curling her nose in distaste.

Karris dropped his voice to a whisper and motioned for Lena to do the same. "Just because your *grandfather* chose to take solace—"

"That has never been proven. Just the word of a poor farm boy and an unreliable servant. Andren was soulbound—"

"Andren was *lonely*. He needed the physical comfort of a willing woman. Though Ellien could never replace—"

"No. She could not."

Karris sighed. It was always like this when Riena's parentage was at issue. The law didn't allow Etan to force Riena's recognition, though it was almost certain that she was who Rosher claimed she was from the first, Lena's aunt by blood.

It was almost a shame that the last Royal incursion into Lena's line was Andren's grandmother—a second cousin to King Evard. Had the alliance been even a generation closer, Riena could not have been claimed in King's Right, and none of this would have transpired in response.

It was a useless argument, and a change of topic was in order. "Since Gerry's—insult was no more than a statement of fact, I cannot grant you leave to kill him."

She threw up her hands in seeming frustration. "Then he—" Lena darkened.

"He what?" Whatever Rosher said or did next was surely what unnerved her most.

"I— He asked if I still wanted to have sex with him, as if I—"

"Do you?" Karris inquired innocently. Secretly, he cheered Rosher's ability to keep her off balance.

As if proving his suspicions, Lena stared off at a point over his shoulder. He smiled widely at that. No man his cousin had met had prepared her for Rosher.

"Lena?" he called. "*Do* you want to?"

She darkened. "Of course—" She hesitated. "Of course not."

"I think you do, and I think you should."

Her brow furrowed at that. "Should?"

"Have sex with him."

"What?" she shouted. "Why?"

"Look at it this way. Gerry knew his words would push you away."

Lena nodded, motioning her hand for him to continue. "And?" she prodded him.

"If you turn away from him, who wins?"

She winced. "He does. Dear Mother." Lena paced around her pallet twice, stopping to shoot Karris a look of pure misery when that was done. "But the games he plays," she complained.

"If you do not have sex with him, who wins?"

Lena nodded and flopped down on her pallet. "Mother take the man."

Karris snorted in laughter. "Most likely."

He went back to his reading, pleased with his performance. Given the challenge, stated so clearly, Lena would never submit. Given Rosher's training in the game, she would be busy for quite some time.

* * * *

Mey 12th, 4015

Caiben pushed open the door to the small outpost, shaking the rain off the folds of his robes with a grimace of distaste. It was no wonder he hadn't left the comforts of the palace since shortly after Karris was born, unless ordered to do so. He'd forgotten how downright uncomfortable it was to spend his days and nights in the rough. The towns were often too far between to find a bed at every moonset and the beds less comfortable than he remembered when he finally arrived.

He spied a Mason Mage, moving uncomfortably, a sure sign that he'd taken lashes for some misdeed. The sound of a chain moving with him made Caiben wince. Whatever this man had done, it had been severe enough to win him both lashes and labor. He decided not to ask.

"How may I be of service, Master...?" The man let the question hang between them.

It didn't surprise Caiben that the Mage didn't recognize him. It wasn't like his youth, the days when far too many people knew who he was. "Caiben," he offered.

The Mason smiled warmly, no doubt glad of a brother Mage who wasn't condemning him for whatever crimes he'd committed. "And what can I do for you, Master Caiben?"

"I am looking for a Mage. A young man traveling. Have any passed this way?"

"Several. And all of them young, some barely old enough to have sealed. Can you tell me more about this Mage you seek?"

Caiben hesitated at that. Etan hadn't wanted him to cause a stir. He hadn't wanted anyone to know that Karris was traveling out of his element. "He traveled with a woman, a royal bodyguard."

"The only royal bodyguard I saw was the one who brought me to justice." He darkened at that, moving his hand as if to hide the chains that bound him to the far wall, while his jailors were away at their rest.

"Was her name Lena?" he asked urgently, hoping he'd found Karris at last.

"I know not her name. I never asked."

He sighed. There was no way to know then. Not unless he caught up with them.

"Do you know where they were headed?"

The Mage shook his head slowly. "I believe they came from Cerse, but I do not know what way they headed when they left here."

"Ridetel or Burselen most likely," he mused. Burselen was more likely. It was less traveled and easier for Karris to hide himself there, if he wished. Caiben turned toward the door, lost in thought.

"Please," the Mason whispered. "Please, pass some time with me. I see no one here. My jailors leave me to tend the night while they rest, and my brother Mages have been sent on to other service. It is raining and chill. I have wine and food. Would you sit with me? Just for an hour or two?"

Caiben turned back in surprise. "Brother Mages?" he asked.

"I was not alone in my crimes, Master. There were three of us. It was a shameful thing, but I will pay my due. We all will."

"What was your crime? What did you do to deserve lashes and chains?"

He lowered his gaze. "We tried to force a traveling Mage into service to end his interference with our trade."

"And?"

"We meant only to frighten them—the boy and his companion, but he attacked in earnest and...it was my blow that the Master saw."

Caiben grimaced. He attacked another Mage both with his magic and physically? "This Mage you struck. He was powerful?" If this fool injured Karris, Etan would have him flayed alive. As long as it wasn't Karris he harmed, he was safe to play out his sentence.

"Yes, Master. Much more powerful than we expected for a Midman."

He groaned. Caiben couldn't imagine Karris hiding as a Midman, but who else would have cause to hide beneath his station? Even Lena would be hard pressed to fight off three Masons in unison. She only carried two thrown blades that he knew of.

"His companion? Was it a woman?"

"Nay, Master Caiben. His companion was a man, a big man who laid blows on one of my brothers in crime before we were caught."

Caiben sighed in relief. It wasn't Karris he'd injured. "Come, Mason Mage. Pour me some wine and let us escape the storm a bit longer."

Chapter Ten

Mey 18th, 4015

Rosher touched the curve of Guard Lena's neck, smiling at her sharply indrawn breath. He trailed his fingers down to her pulse point, noting the increase in her heart rate.

"I see you have decided you still want me," he whispered.

She blushed then nodded silently.

"Even after the things I said?" He laid a kiss at the corner of her jaw, tracing his fingers along her collarbones to her shoulders.

"You...you are not entirely incorrect," Guard Lena offered carefully.

"Is that so?" Rosher replied in amusement.

Was her sex drive actually strong enough to make her admit that she was what he claimed, or was this some sort of game within a game? If that was her game, Guard Lena would find herself teased to aching and left for another seven days. He grimaced. Would almost another week without her touch help his libido or hinder it?

"The Great houses *do* intermarry to strengthen the magic. Daughters in service often *do* mate with their charges. I can deny none of that."

He trailed his hands down her arms, noting the rising chillbumps beneath her tunic. "Indeed, they do. And what am I incorrect about?" There would be something. Guard Lena was not the type of woman who would easily admit complete defeat on any issue, he was certain.

"We balance those bloodlines very carefully to avoid true inbreeding. My mother mated outside the Great houses, as will I. Most likely, my daughters will, as well."

Rosher smiled at her tactful handling. "I stand corrected, Guard Lena." He caressed her stomach.

She shifted against him then stilled, no doubt still uncertain what acts were allowed or forbidden in this game. "You need not call me that."

"Oh, but I must."

"Why?" she whispered.

"As long as you *are* Guard Lena, that is what I shall call you."

"Mayhap I should know what you want of me." She panted out the request, relaxing into his chest with a sigh of pleasure.

"I want you," he replied simply, cupping her hips in his hands and easing her to the proof of that. "I want just you." *And not Guard Lena.*

Rosher winced at how long it would be until he indulged again. Guard Lena was too stubborn to submit to him—at least not quickly. But if she did, the victory would be as sweet for the release he found as it would for—

"Then take what you want," she pleaded.

"Not yet." Rosher teased at the seams that ran along the length of her inner thighs.

Guard Lena groaned at that move. She was apparently very sensitive there. "But—"

He didn't give her time to plead with him. "You have denied your body's call for too long, Guard Lena. It will be quite some time before you are ready for more than loveplay."

126

"Loveplay?" Her voice rose then fell on a moan, as Rosher traced the underside of her breasts to the tips of her erect nipples.

"Do you enjoy what I am doing to you?" he countered. He knew she did. His play was more than play. Rosher was cataloging her most sensitive points, one at a time.

Guard Lena nodded.

"And yet you have never allowed yourself this pleasure." He didn't question it. He didn't have to question it. Her body, like most women's, told him all he needed to know about her sexual preferences.

"But, I—"

Again, he didn't give her time to formulate a counterargument. He needed her mind in the game. Too much thought and planning would only prove a detriment to that. Rosher cupped her breasts in his palms, letting her breathing stimulate them gently for him.

"An example then. You care for Master Caiben?"

She nodded, brushing her forehead into his beard, her breath teasing at his throat.

"Yet you would set that aside, if your orders told you to," he stated confidently. "In the same way, you ignore what your body craves for what seems more insistent at the time."

"No," she denied.

Rosher stroked his fingers from hip to hip, dipping to the center of her mound with the promise of more. Mother, she was so very responsive to a light touch. "Have you ever allowed yourself—"

"Nothing is more important to me than Caiben's safety," she asserted.

He furrowed his brow at that. It wasn't what he'd expected her to say. It wasn't something he'd expected any royal bodyguard to say. Duty was ingrained in them, and nothing came between a royal bodyguard and the orders she was given.

Rosher forced his mind back to the game, pressing Guard Lena to his hips again, his fingertips making slow circles over her heated core. "Even if King—"

"Nothing," she gasped. "Nothing is more important than C—Caiben."

"As nothing should be more important than this," he insisted, thankful that she'd managed to make his point for him, in some strange way.

"Gerry," she pleaded, "I need—"

"I know what you need," he whispered, finding the sensitive spots he'd located in his exploration of her body. "Your body screams for it. Forget what you think you want. I promise you, if the word passes your lips. I will leave you for a full moon passing, no matter how close you are."

"A threat?" she growled.

"Negative reinforcement."

"And if I do not say it?" Her voice was ragged in need, as ragged as his own was becoming.

Rosher bit back a groan at that, at how willing to play his game Guard Lena was proving to be. "Master Caiben spends much of the moon's rising with Romik. They do not need us much of that time, and our other duties are not strenuous."

And he could drive her near mad with a few short days of this treatment. Rosher sobered. He was likely to go mad along with her.

Guard Lena shuddered against him, climaxing almost silently in his arms. Rosher cradled her to his chest, wanting the one thing he could not indulge in anytime soon. He had to draw out her attention as long as he could.

Rosher startled as she turned to him, her hands pulling at his trousers. He stilled them, shaking his head. That was something he could not allow her, or all his plans were forfeit.

"I only want to repay—" Guard Lena grimaced, no doubt noting, as he had, that she had used the forbidden word.

He looked to the moon. "An hour after moonrise tomorrow," he promised.

She grumbled a curse at that.

"Or do you wish our game to end?" he offered, knowing she would glean the challenge to outlast him in it.

Guard Lena stiffened. "An hour after moonrise," she agreed.

Rosher nodded and turned away. "Do not wear your uniform jacket, Guard Lena. It hinders me."

She grunted something that sounded of assent.

As much a relief as it would have been to have her refuse him, he was somehow glad she wouldn't.

* * * *

Mey 22nd, 4015

Caiben knocked at the door, hoping the farmer within was awake at this hour. His search was slowed considerably by dealing with night-sleepers. The farmers Karris was most likely to have interacted with would rarely be awake for more than four hours past moonrise and two before moonset.

That left a full nine hours of the night during which Caiben could only travel and go to inns that catered to both night-sleepers and Mages, in the slim hope that Karris had ventured there. So far, none of the inns he'd checked had seen anything of a young Mage traveling with a royal bodyguard. As he'd warned Etan, finding Karris was much more difficult than finding his father had ever proven.

The door opened, and a grizzled old farmer nodded to Caiben. "Good moonrise, Master. I am sorry, but I have just had my fields tended by your brother Mages. I have no work for you."

"I have not come searching for work. I seek a Mage, a young Mage traveling with a royal bodyguard. Have you seen him?"

The man seemed to consider that carefully. "Mayhap."

Caiben groaned at that. What would it be? A bribe to learn the information he sought? A bit of magic to win his tongue loose? "Mayhap?" he asked, giving the farmer time to make his request.

"Well, there were two Mages that passed through with a mated couple who served them. The woman had the look of a former bodyguard or soldier of some sort, if you know what I mean."

"I do not," Caiben answered, honestly perplexed. A bodyguard never left service.

The farmer motioned him inside, setting out a mug of ale for each of them before he spoke again. "She wore the polished boots and trousers of a bodyguard, and her manner was stiff, except with her man, but she wore no uniform jacket or other mark of rank. She was serious, that one—except with her man."

"You say they were a mated couple?" Caiben asked, unwilling to disregard any clue that might lead him to Karris.

"I would say they were. Bold as you please. I came across them more than once, engaging in loveplay in the woods near their camp."

"Definitely not." Lena was discreet about her lovers. This group couldn't be the ones he sought. It was another cold trail. Caiben sighed, draining the mug of ale. "My thanks for your help." He dropped two silver coins on the table for the drink and the man's trouble.

The farmer smiled. "What name may I praise when I pray to the Mother this moonrise, Master?" he offered. "For your health and for your quest to come to a happy end?"

He smiled. "That is a kind wish. My name is Caiben, sir."

"Guyben," he offered with a nod.

"Caiben." He grimaced at the misstep with his name.

"Guyben," the farmer repeated.

Caiben furrowed his brow. Was the man hard of hearing? He repeated the name again.

"I beg your indulgence, fine Master, but I must have misheard either you or the other."

"The other?"

"I have met a Mage I thought was named Caiben, and I assure you, it was not you. But I have met many men in my long years. I suppose all the names sound alike, after a time."

Caiben bowed his head reverently and left with a laugh of delight. He'd been well-known through these parts in his younger years. Mayhap Caiben had tumbled this old man's daughter. He sighed at that, casting one more look back. Mayhap it was his granddaughter.

Chapter Eleven

Mey 26th, 4015

"Damn the man," Lena cursed.

Karris chuckled at that, shielding his eyes until she closed the flap and blocked the sunlight. "Problem, little cousin?" He knew there was, but Karris enjoyed seeing Lena so frustrated. Mayhap because she shared in his pain. Lena could not touch Rosher, as Karris could not touch Riena.

"Little? I am less than a month your junior," she reminded him.

"Gerry still denies you?" he asked.

"Mother take him," she grumbled.

"What would you have me do? Reveal myself to him and order him to lay with you?"

Lena was silent for a long moment, her breathing harsh in the stillness around them.

Karris chuckled again. "So, the mighty Guard Lena has fallen at last," he mused.

"Do not call me that," she snapped.

"Call you what?"

She sighed. "*Guard* Lena."

"I see."

"Do you?" Her voice had lost its edge. Lena sounded lost and alone.

"I believe so. You have been Guard Lena so long that you have forgotten how to be anything else." He scowled. "And Guard Lena is not what Gerry wants of you."

As Romik wasn't what Karris wanted. As Prince Karris wasn't what Riena wanted. Dear

Mother, this whole thing was maddening! He only hoped that Riena cared for "Master Caiben."

Lena collapsed to her pallet with a sigh. "You understand," she conceded.

"Yes. I do understand." Karris did understand. Working with Riena, sharing in her channeling, watching her, smelling her, wanting her and not being able to have her would likely drive him insane before he figured out how best to approach her.

"I do not understand what Gerry wants of me," she complained.

Karris considered that carefully. Mayhap their dilemmas were not far removed. "Mayhap Gerry wants to know you. Not the guard you are when you need to be but *you*."

He held out a faint glimmer of hope that Riena simply needed to know him. Not Prince Karris but Karris, the man he was behind the crown he wore on public occasions, the man beyond the King's Right that made her fear and hate him. If that were true, and Riena got to know the man he was, she wouldn't try to escape him when he revealed himself to her.

"Karris?" she whispered.

"Caiben," he reminded her. It had been well over a month, and Lena still needed reminded to use his assumed name in private. If Riena discovered his identity before he revealed himself, she would run. He had no doubts.

"Caiben?"

"What is it, Lena?"

"How do I know who I am when I am not Guard Lena?"

He stroked his chin, a nervous habit he'd inherited from his father. "When you stop acting for the sake of others and follow your heart, you are truly yourself."

* * * *

Rosher curled onto his pallet, cursing the state of arousal he'd been left in again. He listened to Riena's even breathing, glad that she wasn't awake to question him, that he wasn't forced to offer lies about his interest in Lena.

Remembering to call her Guard Lena was becoming more difficult every night. But, now he was alone again, unable to touch her for another passing. *Why did she have to say it?* Four encounters out of five, that damned word issued forth. *Lena.* Every time he thought she'd abandoned the idea of telling him what she wanted, she uttered the word again and drove him away.

When would Lena realize that Rosher gave her exactly what she indicated by her motions, scent, and sounds without being ordered to do so? When would she see how aroused that made him? He knew exactly how to touch her. Was a man who could do that without being ordered to do it a detriment? One would think Lena would be glad to reap enjoyment without having to maintain a draining dialog. Without being forced out of pure bliss to think and decide and direct—

And now Lena had said it again. Rosher cursed aloud at that. They'd had time to finish what he'd started with her and play another round. Now he would be forced to suffer until nearly moonset tomorrow.

He couldn't go to her early. Or could he? It would keep Lena off balance if he did. Rosher bit back a groan, admitting the painful truth to himself that he would hide from Riena at all costs.

What would keep Lena off balance had ceased to matter to Rosher, at some indeterminate point during the game. No one but Guard Dera had managed to win this single-minded fascination from him. He wanted her. Every time she placed herself in his hands, Rosher wanted to end the game, to give Lena the prize she sought.

He couldn't put off that step much longer. All too soon, he would surrender to the heat of the moment. Rosher prayed to the Mother that Lena wouldn't proclaim her victory by turning from him—and that he wouldn't surrender the fight the next time they played at each other.

The only solace he could offer himself was that Lena would have no idea that she'd bested the infamous Rosher of Bentin, guard crusher, when he finally fell to her.

* * * *

Mey 27th, 4015

Lena bit her lip, letting the bucket in her hand ease to the ground as Gerry cupped his hands beneath her breasts. His thumbs played at the points of her nipples, and her body came to life. He laid a kiss under the corner of her jaw, a sure sign that he was pleased with her response.

She laid her head back into the slight hollow of his shoulder, riding the waves of pleasure making her knees tremble. Lena gasped his name, pushing the question of what he was doing here out of her mind. He was early. She hadn't expected Gerry for four more hours, but that was less important than the magic he worked on her body and mind.

"Lean into me," he instructed.

She obeyed without question. Gerry rarely spoke to her when he played this game. When he did, whatever he suggested was certain to increase her enjoyment.

His body was taut in excitement, like a viper ready to strike. His member was hard and his hand insistent.

Lena rolled her head, her eyes closing as her womb throbbed in time with Gerry's touch. The feelings were too intense. "Please," she begged, unable to stand much more of this torture.

"Let go for me, Lena. I can feel how close you are. Your body has wanted this your whole life."

"I w—" She clenched her jaw to stop the damned word that always made him walk away. Tonight, she would not utter it.

Gerry groaned, his fingers playing her like a gittine, strumming and plucking at her sensitized flesh until music filled her ears.

"Very good, Lena. I know what you need. You are so close to it. Let your body sing, and I promise you will have what you want most."

Lena fisted her hands, her breathing ragged. Nay. She would not have what she wanted. She wanted more than this delicious game. She wanted the man who mastered her body to become her mate, but Lena feared that all there was for Gerry was the game.

She forced her mind away from that and to his possession of her. He'd promised her an end to her waiting. Visions of Gerry's body pounding into hers overlapped with the powerful sensations of his loveplay. Her mouth was abruptly dry, and a cry of longing escaped her lips.

Everything seemed to happen at once. One of Gerry's hands left her breast and pulled open her trousers. As his fingers found her core, she shattered, crying out again as her body spasmed against his hands.

Gerry eased her to her knees, cradled in the shelter of his body. He trembled, his fingertips still lightly breaching her body. "You will have me, Lena."

Aftershocks wracked her body at that. She couldn't form the words to praise the Mother—or to beg for mercy, which some irrational part of her mind screamed for.

Lena barely noted that her clothing was disappearing before she was nude beneath Gerry's body, skin to skin with him for the first time. His length eased inside her, and her body seemed to burn, incinerating in pleasure that bordered on pain. This was what Karris told her channeling a standard rebirth felt like.

She licked her lips, her body moving against his, her skin seemingly as sensitive as a Star Mage's. His hair felt like silk against her stomach and chest, and his member moved like a heated spoon through cream, stirring waves of steam and igniting her again. Lena screamed in a combination of delight and surprise as he pushed her past endurance again.

Gerry stilled, his expression fiercely possessive as he joined her in that moment of the Mother's Death. Then he filled her, and colors danced before her eyes.

Rebirth, she noted dimly. *No wonder Mother Moon does this every season.*

Gerry laid a kiss on her lips, his smile smug and his body relaxed. "Was it worth waiting for?" he teased.

Lena laughed at his audacity. "Will you make me wait again if I say nay?"

"Most assuredly." He propped his chin on his elbow, his eyes glittering in the high moon. "As you might assume, the rules of engagement have changed slightly."

He chuckled, rolling away and tumbling Lena over him as she smacked his arm.

Chapter Twelve

Mey 30th, 4015

Karris reached his hand out, cradling it beneath Riena's, both anticipating and dreading the channeling to come. His anticipation was a simple thing to reason. Her fire was so pure and powerful, it stole his breath to lend aid to it.

There was no question that it was Karris lending strength and Riena channeling the flow, her slight form communing with the Mother in a way he could only dream of doing. It was uncertain if Riena realized she was the focal point. So much about her use of the magic seemed to elude her notice, an automatic process for her, instinctive rather than learned. Mayhap all female Star Mages were endowed with such a gift. Mayhap that was how she'd survived the Silver Minute that brought her to him.

His dread was less clear to him. On one hand, simply admitting that not being able to touch Riena as he longed to do was driving him mad. Sharing in the channeling, he shared her arousal. Every time Riena slipped into climax, it was a battle for him not to join her. Twice, he *had* joined her, something he had never done in solitary or even in shared channeling—until Riena.

On the other, it was much more complex than that. Every channeling left Karris deeper in fear that someone would discover their secrets. Whether someone recognized Karris or saw Riena for a woman, Etan would descend upon them, and Riena would hate him at the moment when Karris believed she might be beginning to trust and like him.

He looked to Riena, cursing himself for forgetting she waited for his signal to begin. It was a lesson hailing back to his earliest training. The strongest almost always led. With his teachers, Karris had followed until he sealed. With his father, Karris deferred, the only time he had altered the rule until Riena came into his life.

Karris expected Riena to lead, by virtue of her power. His mind and soul anticipated her lead, but Riena had never been permitted to lead a shared channeling, always kept under strict control of the masters who'd taught her, in hopes that she would defer to Karris in the same way he deferred to his father.

"Now," he instructed her.

Riena's power passed over his hand and coiled like a serpent around his scarred wrist, playing over the proof of his identity he kept carefully hidden. All of Voria knew the story of the female Mage who'd marked him in a duel. They whispered of it in awe, sending children to sleep with images of the terrible power the "she-Mage" wielded.

As Riena had to hide her gender, Karris had to hide himself in Master's black and a braceband. One close look at those scars and someone would whisper of having seen the "Scarred Black Prince" in a child's bedchamber that night.

Karris blushed at Riena's questioning look. His inattention would cost them more than the pay for this channeling. It could cost him Riena's continued presence in his camp.

He cleared his mind, forcing his thoughts to the channeling. Like a lightening fork, the magic shot from Karris, tangling with Riena's and drowning him in the rush of power.

His senses opened fully. He closed his eyes to the too-bright night sky. His hearing locked onto one sound after another: the whisper of wind around them, the shift of soil beneath the farmer's boots, Riena's sharp intake of breath, and their hearts beating in time to the pulse of magic coursing through them. The smell of Riena's rising musk, the sweat on her upturned face, pure female essence played on his frayed nerves.

Karris pushed away errant images of pressing his lips to hers and tasting the magic on her body, stealing the fragrance of power unleashed from her skin. He focused instead on the flow of power, examining Riena's work, marveling at her expertise.

There was a sudden shift, and Karris focused his full attention on the changing flow. He opened his eyes a slit, looking to Riena, considering her intentions. She wasn't forcing growth anymore but rather healing something. Karris followed the flow of power, gauging its purpose carefully.

As if feeling his intrusion, Riena's hand moved within his, stroking his sealing scars. Karris panted back a fierce wave of pleasure at that. Would that Riena would touch those scars as palace bed servants sometimes did, he would die a happy man.

Rosher moved forward, catching Riena as she slipped over into climax. Karris ground his teeth, weaving on his feet and grasping at Lena's shoulder. He shuddered, controlling the need to follow Riena into bliss...but only just.

"Are you well?" Lena whispered.

Karris nodded. Oh, yes. He was well. His body was alive and aware of his needs as a man.

Riena sent a weak smile to Rosher, nodding away a similar question.

"Well done," Farmer Gaultin thundered, reaching to clap a hand on Riena's shoulder.

Rosher shifted her away from the burly farmer's touch, a seemingly accidental move, but Karris knew better. Things like that could see their doom. Karris tensed, then threw out a hand to still Lena as she reached for her weapon, his reaction sending her into automatic reaction.

"The coin, if you please," Karris requested, giving Gaultin something to draw his mind from the strange reactions of the group of Mages and companions.

The farmer furrowed his brow, moving his gaze from Riena to Karris. "As you wish, Master Caiben. Are you certain you will not grace my home for the day? My wife has prepared a meal for—"

"Thank you. Nay. I am fatigued and require the solace of my light blocking tent." *And a safe haven from your three grasping daughters.*

"Mayhap Midman Romik—"

"Nay," Karris replied shortly, saving Riena the trouble of making her own excuses. "The Midman has studies to attend to this night."

One of the three daughters put on a pout that most Mages probably found endearing. She'd chosen the wrong two Mages this night. Riena certainly had no interest in the women's attentions, and Karris found his interest riveted to Riena.

Even were it not, this Vorian Heir would hardly tumble a farmer's daughter unless he planned to take her to mate, no matter what mad scrapes his father had gotten himself into before he took Sabina to mate. Karris winced at that, at the stories still whispered by servants about his father's carefree days. They had always expected Karris to fall close to that mark, but Karris wasn't Etan, and since he had no plans to take one of Gaultin's daughters as his mate, they were doomed to sate themselves with village men until the next Mages passed through.

Gaultin scowled, then bowed his bushy head. "As the Master wishes. I will send the coin and food to your camp within the hour."

Karris ground his teeth at that but held his words tightly, bowing his agreement and turning away. Rosher turned with him, keeping Riena's back as Lena kept his.

The night was cool and bright, a light breeze teasing at their hair in promise of a good growing season.

At their camp, Karris nodded Riena into his tent and waved their guards away to what had quickly become their main pastime when they weren't needed.

Riena didn't hesitate. Taking his comment about her studies firmly to heart, Riena sat with *The Master's Words* on her lap when he followed her inside. Karris stretched out on his pallet and watched her, considering the chance of failure they wrestled with daily.

"Why did you heal the diseased crops?" he asked. "We were not hired to do more than bring growth."

Riena didn't look up. She darkened, clearing her throat. "Should we not serve—"

"Why did you not tell Gaultin and receive payment for our services?" he interrupted her.

"He would believe we'd deceived him. Gaultin likely didn't know the mist lace was even there and might not have until almost harvest time." Riena explained her point simply and without question that it was so.

Karris nodded his agreement. No doubt the farmer would have believed that very thing. "You could have stopped and—" He faltered as her head snapped up, her eyes wide. "What is it?"

She seemed to consider her answer carefully, weighing each word. "If I had done so, he would believe us greedy, grasping—" Riena looked back to the great book. "We cannot serve where there is no trust, Caiben. Can we?

"Now Gaultin will have a healthy crop and remember us fondly. Whether I refused to treat the problem and pretended not to know or sought payment, I would have undermined his trust in us—and in all Mages."

Karris leaned forward, sensing something more, something she wasn't saying. "And?" he prodded.

She scooped a lock of hair behind her ear, a nervous habit, much as his stroking his chin was. "His children will eat this winter, Caiben. Gaultin might have refused my healing in anger, had I asked it of him. Another Mage might not have passed through. He might not have had the extra coin to pay us—or another Mage to do the job. He might not have discovered the damage until a quarter of his crops were destroyed by it. If the children eating means a bit of my help, I offer it freely."

"Even if you do not eat as well?" he asked carefully.

Riena shrugged. "I do well enough. If the few weeks before planting are lean, I will survive them."

"You have gone hungry," he guessed. Why had he never reasoned that? Karris knew she'd been cast out, that she'd day-labored to survive, night to night.

She didn't answer, staring at the great book as if hypnotized by it.

"Romik?"

"Yes?" Her voice was far away, as if she were distracted...or avoiding him.

"You have gone hungry." He annunciated each word, stressing his demand for an answer without saying so.

"Yes. I have." It was said without emotion, a fact of her life. Karris swallowed hard, aching to hold her. He'd never known hunger or cold. The scars she'd left on him were the most pain he'd ever felt—until he sealed, and his only fear was failing her—losing her. He would lose her if he pulled her to his chest as he longed to do.

"You may go, Romik. You did well, and you should rest."

Riena looked up, seemingly torn, her hand pressed to the page she was reading. "May I take the great book with me, Caiben?"

"You may rest," he reminded her. "It is not necessary—"

"Please. I would like to study a bit longer." She looked on the verge of tears, though she held herself firmly in control, not spilling a drop down her soft cheeks.

Karris nodded. "Of course, but promise me you will rest soon."

Riena offered him a wide smile that threatened to tip the tears from her lashes. "My vow."

* * * *

Riena stepped into the night air, *The Master's Words* pressed to her chest. She bit back a laugh. *Free!* The knowledge Caiben gifted her might set her free. Free of Etan and Karris. Free to live her life as she saw fit to. Free to take a mate of her own choice.

She crossed the clearing to her tent, a smile etched on her face. The knowledge was half the battle. Now Riena had to decide how best to *use* the knowledge she'd been denied all these years.

"Finish the book," she whispered. There could be no mistakes. Riena would read every page of the great book, every law. Once she knew all there was to know—

Riena startled at the touch on her arm, turning to face the person who came at her with such stealth and dared touch her. She scowled at the sight of Gaultin's youngest daughter.

Riena knew the type well. Duria was a fair young face accustomed to the Mother's most superficial gifts buying her whatever favors she wished from men. Like a Blue Lady, there wasn't much substance to women like Duria, and her pretty exterior was easily torn away.

Riena opened her mouth to order the young woman away. With the rushing speed of the Silver Minute, Duria closed the distance between them, her mouth closing over Riena's, her tongue delving inside.

Riena gagged, ripping her mouth away, forcing herself not to lose her early meal. "How dare you," she managed in controlled fury.

Duria tried to press her body to Riena's again, her brow furrowing as she encountered the shield of the great book between them.

Riena braced her body away with a hand on the taller woman's shoulder. "I gave you no leave to touch me. Do not attempt that again." She had to keep her temper in check. Duria's horrid behavior accounted for, it wouldn't do to alienate Gaultin.

The farmer's daughter smiled a sly smile, looking to where a male member would lie beneath her robes if Riena were male. "I wish only to bring you ease," she offered.

"Your touch, no slight intended, brings no ease when work beckons."

"It would relax you for the work," Duria reasoned stubbornly, her lip protruding in a pout that turned Riena's stomach.

Duria's hand shot out with the speed of a viper strike, a blur of motion aimed for Riena's crotch. She recoiled, turning to ensure that Duria came away with only a handful of robe and not a bushel of information that Riena didn't want her to have. Riena pushed her away roughly, her calm fleeing at Duria's abrupt motion.

"I told you not to touch me," she thundered. "There are punishments for—" She ducked another touch, this one aimed for her cheek.

"Let me give you ease," Duria purred. Her amorous look fled, replaced by a look of biting fury as Caiben's hand closed around her extended wrist and jerked her around to face him. "How dare you," she began coldly.

Caiben's face was a mass of taut lines, a deadly look Riena had never seen on him before. "I dare less than you do," he growled. His gaze didn't leave Duria's face. "Are you well, Romik?"

Riena took a calming breath. "Well enough. Thank you, Master."

He nodded, his long hair brushing over his bare chest and shoulders. "I trust you are here to deliver the coin for your father, young daughter." Caiben didn't question it, as if he'd expected something like this to happen.

Duria sighed, tossing the bag to Caiben as if hoping he would release her to catch it. Her wish was destined to go ungranted.

Caiben snatched the bag with his free hand without losing her gaze. He pushed her away lightly. "You will leave our camp and not return," he demanded in a quiet voice that held the promise of death.

"You are still on my father's land," she countered, nursing disappointment at what was probably her first failure with a man she wanted to seduce.

Riena grimaced at an unwelcome spike of jealousy that coursed through her. Would Duria have succeeded if she'd pursued Caiben and not Riena? Her gaze traveled the smooth expanse of Caiben's chest. Likely, she would have succeeded.

Riena swallowed a bitter lump. She couldn't prevent that. If Caiben chose to bed a farmer's daughter, there was nothing Riena could do but stop her ears to the sounds of their passion and nurse her hurt that it wasn't herself in Caiben's bed, that it could *never* be her in Caiben's bed.

She looked to the great book, biting her lower lip. Or could it be? She had to finish reading to be certain.

Caiben laughed shortly, reminding Riena that there was still the matter of Duria to be dealt with.

"Would your father prefer the discomfort of our company for the next two days, as he promised, or knowing you took the lash for daring to touch Midman Romik when ordered away?" His voice clearly announced that Caiben wouldn't hesitate to have her lashed.

Duria turned on her heel, prepared to storm away. "Wait," Caiben called. "Take your sisters with you, if you please."

Riena gasped, stiffening her spine as the flap to her tent moved and Gaultin's older daughters slipped out, their heads bowed, blushing lightly.

Caiben grunted, his face now announcing his disgust with this farce. "I imagine they intended to share you, Romik."

She bit back a groan at the thought of trying to fight off all three women. Another thought added to her discomfort. A vision of Caiben surrounded by their ample young bodies, trading touches and kisses, made her head swim.

Caiben's warm hand stroked her cheek. "You are pale. Are you sure you are well?"

Riena nodded, weaving slightly and grasping at Caiben's arm for balance. "I am," she lied.

Duria snorted in disgust. "You will regret this night," she vowed. "Both of you will."

Caiben pulled Riena to his chest as she shivered. "We will send our companions for the food," he shouted after them. "You need not trouble yourself with bringing it to us."

Riena pressed her forehead to Caiben's chest. It would be over all too soon. If Duria brought attention to them, Riena would have to flee, knowledge or no.

She sighed as Caiben's arms wrapped around her. Mayhap the great book's knowledge could win her this reality instead of the one she was ordered to, if she learned how to use that knowledge quickly enough.

Chapter Thirteen

Mey 32nd, 4015

Caiben sighed, scanning his eyes about the small inn. He'd stayed in worse over the years, though not since he'd found himself in a duel with a rash young prince in disguise and entered Etan's service after several days of heavy drinking with Etan and Andrel. Caiben furrowed his brow, thinking back to that time, almost four decades earlier. Was he in Ridetel? This inn had the look of the one they'd passed those drunken days in, beset by willing young women.

As if answering his unasked question, there was a willing young woman at his side, her hands tracing his wrist to the sensitive scars on his palm in unspoken offer.

He chuckled. It had been years since he'd indulged with a barmaid or a farmer's daughter. Caiben took her measure. This one had experience enough to make the remaining night memorable. Her eyes held the promise of that.

"What is your name, girl?"

She smiled. "Duria, daughter of Gaultin Boret, Master." Caiben nodded to the barkeep and accepted a room key, leading Duria to the room supplied for them.

He'd only intended to stop for mid meal and to ask more questions that would surely prove useless, but who could refuse such a temptation? Caiben had been without the comfort of royal bed servants for almost a month, traveling long hours with no return, dispirited and uncomfortable.

Surely, Etan wouldn't begrudge him this small measure of comfort.

Duria wasted no time, carefully parting his robes and inviting his kiss. Caiben smiled at that. It seemed this farmer's daughter wished to ravage him. Who was Caiben to deny them both that delight?

She pulled off his robes, setting them aside with a hungry look. Duria drew his hand up, stroking her lips over his sealing scars. Caiben's body reacted fiercely to that, his arousal nearly maddening.

"Yes," she urged him, cupping his ready length through his trousers. "You are a *true* Star Mage."

Something in that comment niggled at Caiben. His pursuit of relaxation aside, he was seeking a Mage, and Karris had a history of irritating the softer sex. It was his duty to make certain it wasn't Karris she'd seen.

Caiben pressed a kiss to the smooth skin of her cheek. "Another Mage has come this way?" he asked.

Her hands wandered beneath his tunic, tracing the length of his stomach. "Two," she confirmed.

"Together?"

Duria scowled. "Yes."

Caiben smiled at that, reaching for the buttons on her dress. It couldn't be Karris, but it was likely the pair who'd been to several farms he'd questioned recently. If it was not Karris, Caiben was free to pursue his pleasure for a few moments more.

"Master Caiben," she growled.

He chuckled. Had his reputation survived this long? "Yes?" he asked.

"I mean no disrespect," she whispered.

Caiben looked to her in confusion. "What disrespect?"

Duria met his eyes, looking equally perplexed. "Master Caiben."

"Yes?" he asked again, waving for her to say her peace and be done with it before irritation stole the last of his arousal.

"My pardons, Master. I should not speak ill of one of your brother Mages."

He started to nod.

"Even when that Mage is that insufferable beast, Master Caiben."

Caiben's breath caught in his chest. Karris wouldn't dare— An image of Etan, a barmaid on each knee in the common room below, flashed through his mind. Karris *would* dare, though no one else would.

"Master Caiben was here?" he asked urgently.

I have met a Mage I thought was named Caiben, and I assure you, it was not you.

Dear mother, have I had Karris in my sights this whole time?

"Did I not say that?" She seemed genuinely uncertain.

"With another Mage?"

There were two Mages that passed through with a mated couple who served them.

"His student, Midman Romik," she confirmed.

Caiben laughed aloud.

The only royal bodyguard I saw was the one who brought me to justice.

It was my blow that the Master saw.

Much more powerful than we expected for a Midman.

It was ingenious! Karris knew they would be looking for a Mage traveling alone. He'd picked up his Midman at the farms outside of Cerse and traveled as a master and student to attract less notice. Caiben had to be certain.

"He had a guard with him?"

"Two. Midman Romik's companion and a royal bodyguard for Master Caiben."

The boy and his companion. His companion was a man, a big man.

A mated couple who served them.

Caiben laughed heartily. "Where did that young fool go?"

Duria darkened, her eyes wide. "You know of Master Caiben?"

"Oh, I know him. Better than I care to admit, sometimes." Who would have guessed that Karris had so much of his father in him, after all? "Where have they gone?" *Mother Moon, please let her know their route. If I find Karris, I can return to the palace.*

"To Olt," she stammered.

Caiben nodded. "How long ago were they here?"

"They left only this moonrise."

He grumbled a curse, snatching up his robes and dragging them over his shoulders.

"Master?" she asked, half stunned by his outburst.

"I must go. If I go now, I may catch them before moonset." He laid one hard kiss on her lips.

"My vow. I will return this way soon, and my— payment for this information may well leave you exhausted."

A vengeful look lit her face. "You seek Master Caiben?" she asked excitedly.

"I do." He fastened his robes over his untucked tunic.

"Is he— Will he be sanctioned for some misdeed?" her eyes glittered at that.

Caiben wondered what Karris had done to anger Duria. "One could say that," he answered carefully. Etan was hardly amused by his son's disappearance, his robes abandoned at Riena's home. There would be sanction for it. There was no doubt of that.

Duria placed a quick kiss on his cheek and turned Caiben toward the corridor, seemingly speeding him to Karris's doom.

He ignored the snickers on the way through the main room. There would be whispers of the Master Mage who'd tumbled Duria with the speed of a lightening fork later this night and for many nights to come.

At his mount, Duria smoothed his robes. "I shall wait word of your return, Master, but what name shall I harking to?"

He touched her cheek again, leaning close to her ear so none might overhear what he would say. "Master Caiben," he whispered.

She half-swallowed a squeak of surprise, and her eyes went wide.

"Shhh. Tell no one. If this imposter hears whispers of my approach, he will evade me."

Caiben brushed his lips over hers in farewell. "And that would delay my return to you."

Duria laughed harshly. "I have no love for Mas—for the fiend. Whatever brings him to justice soonest, I will do."

Caiben nodded and mounted his horse, urging the beast to a run without a backward glance. If Mother Moon was kind, he would finish what he started with Duria before the night of the Grand Rebirth.

Caiben rode hard for hours, eating up the leagues toward Olt as fast as he dared. Moonset was approaching when he saw the encampment at last.

He came at them by stealth, watching the couple by the fireside from the shadows. It was just as the Mason Mage and the old farmer had described it. Lena wore a tunic and trousers with her guard boots, but she was without her uniform jacket. She was playing love-struck maid in a way most unlike herself, taking bits of fruit from the hand of the huge golden man, casting him amorous looks, and pulling him over her playfully as if she would take his body next to the open fire.

Caiben raised an eyebrow at that. This night was no end of surprises.

He stepped out, noting that neither Lena nor the Midman's companion noticed his presence in light of their preoccupation with each other. "Guard Lena," Caiben called sweetly, crossing his arms over his chest.

Her head turned, and Lena paled, stilling the man poised over her with a shaking hand. She urged the companion aside and sat up, brushing her mussed hair away from her face.

Caiben nodded at that. "Where is he?" he demanded.

* * * *

Karris grimaced at the voice outside. It was a voice he'd never forget, and unless he acted quickly, it would be a voice that spelled his doom with Riena.

"Where is he?" Caiben repeated. His voice was losing what little patience he'd shown the first time.

"Who is it?" Riena whispered, trying hard to mask her terror.

"Stay here," Karris answered. "He is an old master who is full of himself. Nothing more." He left the tent without giving her a chance to question him further, praying he could turn Caiben aside.

The Palace Master's eyes scanned over Karris's black robes, devoid of amusement. "I assume you have something to say to me?" he prompted.

Karris stiffened his spine, reminding himself that Caiben had been his lesser for five years. He motioned to Rosher's back with his eyes then to the forest with his hand. "Walk with me," he invited.

Caiben nodded and preceded him to the edge of the trees, sending a curt bow toward Lena and Rosher. Karris motioned the two guards to Riena, then followed Caiben away from the fire. The light had faded completely away before Caiben broke their silence.

"Your student and his guard have no idea who you are," he noted.

"Nay, they do not, and I have no intentions of letting them discover it. Teaching Romik affords me cover and an air of respectability."

He'd argued this with himself many times. Karris was lying to Riena, but doing so would safeguard her until he found a way to approach her with the truth. There were no guarantees of what her reaction to his true identity might be. He couldn't risk her running in fear, no matter that the cost of it was the perpetuation of this lie.

There were worse things than a lie. As long as Riena traveled with Karris, he could guard her from nearly all of them. Mayhap he would find a way to guarantee her trust soon. He would have to find a way. His time was coming to an end.

The old man sighed, pushing his silver-shot hair away from his face. "You must return to your father. He demands—"

"I cannot. Not yet."

"Karris—"

"I am tracking her, Caiben. Always, I am a day behind, mere hours from touching her. Riena is not running from me yet. She has no concept of how close I am to her. If I contact my father, every guard will know where I am and what I seek. Whispers will precede me. I will never have what I seek then. Would you rather see Riena at my father's mercy than mine?"

Caiben grumbled a curse. "Nay. You know I would not. If there is any chance you might find her first— Mayhap your father will forgive me, if I travel with you."

"Nay. Two masters traveling together would cause talk." He forced a smile to his face. "Besides, there cannot be *two* Master Caibens. What name would you use?"

"Why did you pick *my* name?" he asked, no doubt irritated by Karris's teasing.

Karris raised an eyebrow at that. "You have not left the palace outside of the company of my father or myself in a decade or more."

"More," he snapped. "Much more."

"How was I to know you would choose now—"

"I hardly chose to come. Your father ordered me to find you."

Karris bit back a groan at that. "You were the only master I felt certain I would not encounter. Nor would anyone I was likely to meet remember your face. I am capable of avoiding Great Mages and Masters, and what others would know you? What other name was available to me?"

Caiben didn't answer that.

An uneasy lurch nearly unseated Karris's late meal. "How did you find me?"

The Master winced.

"You told someone who I am." Karris muttered a curse.

"Nay," Caiben answered quietly.

"Then what?"

"I met a farmer's daughter—"

"You?" Karris laughed. "You tumbled—"

"Nay!" But, his pale cheeks were touched with color.

Karris stepped before him and stared Caiben down. He grasped a fold of Caiben's robes and inhaled, smiling at the trace of female musk. Karris cleared his throat, fingering the robes and demanding an answer silently.

"Very well," Caiben snapped, pulling his robes from Karris's hand and smoothing them with a crimson face and eyes that didn't quite meet his prince's. "I had *intended* to tumble her, until she mentioned a rather unpleasant meeting with Master Caiben. I knew no one but you would dare take my name."

"And what did you tell her?" That was the most important thing to know. If Caiben told this maid who Karris was—or even hinted at it, he would have to reveal himself to Riena and plead her forgiveness for his deception this very night.

And she will flee. By the Mother, I cannot permit that.

"That you were an imposter to my name, and I would take you to justice. I would not worry. Duria—"

"Duria, daughter of Gaultin Boret," he groaned. "You have ruined me."

Caiben ran a hand through his hair. "Not necessarily."

Karris motioned for him to continue. Any chance was better than the certainty that Duria's story would reach the wrong ears all too soon.

"I promised to return to her and reward her for her help—in a most intimate fashion. I could make it a rather prolonged encounter. Would her father protest such a thing?"

He snorted. "Would most fathers?"

Except Riena's grandfather, though by all accounts, Telan only balked at the liaison, because bearing Andren's child cost Ellien her life. Would that his precious Ellien had lived, Riena would have had a very different life indeed. One without hunger.

"Nay. Farmer Gaultin will not protest such an arrangement. How long can you win her silence?"

Caiben laughed harshly. "Unless I have grown far too old, I can win you until the Grand Rebirth, easily."

Karris clasped Caiben's shoulder. "Not so easily, old friend."

"How so?"

"Duria has two older sisters, and they are not adverse to the idea of sharing a Mage."

Caiben grimaced. "Are you certain I cannot pass the day? Or two? I need not return to her quite that quickly. It would look—"

"Nay. I have little time, Caiben. Any further complications would be most unwelcome. Waste the day elsewhere if you wish, but do not announce your name overmuch."

Caiben sighed, nodding his agreement. "Will the Grand Rebirth be long enough?" he asked.

"I will have to make it be, Caiben." But how would he convince Riena to trust him so quickly?

Chapter Fourteen

Juno 7th, 4015

She is not immune to me, Karris argued with himself silently. He'd been watching Riena carefully since Caiben left, praying for signs that she trusted him. What he saw encouraged him. Riena's gaze touched his body often and lingered, as if she longed to touch but feared what Karris would find if invited to touch in return.

He wondered if touch might bring her to him. Touch was a powerful motivator for Mages, a link so strong that it could bind the soul when done at the right time—in the right way.

At the very least, she would know a gentle touch from him if they were caught.

In retrospect, their first meeting had been a disaster of sorts. It was no wonder Riena feared taking "Prince Karris" to her bed.

Karris sighed at that. Touch or some other method, he had to try something new. His time was limited. If there was any chance of Riena turning to him in trust, Karris would have to achieve it soon, but how best to accomplish that without frightening her away from him?

Riena rubbed a hand over the back of her neck, and Karris bit back a smile. Touch it was. He stopped pacing and sank to his knees behind her, kneading Riena's shoulders. She stiffened and started to pull away, gasping in surprise.

"Nay," Karris breathed. "Let me ease your pain. Let me touch you."

She stilled, her arms close over her breasts, curled in on herself. Her breathing came in slow, deep, forced breaths.

He nodded and started massaging her sore muscles again. "Be calm," he whispered. "I mean you no harm."

Riena's eyes closed, and she unknotted in his hands. Her breathing became more choppy. Karris moved his hands to her neck, her throat, then her face, moving around her slowly as he worked. Her eyes remained closed. That was probably a good thing. The fierce arousal burning in Karris was surely etched onto his face for all to see. That would send Riena running from him.

He eased her stronger hand up, stroking his fingertips over her sealing scars. Riena gasped, her female musk intensifying as he knew it would. The urge to brush his lips over the scars was nearly overpowering. He touched them again instead.

She pulled back at his hold, her eyes wide but not quite meeting his, fisting her hand and shaking her head as if begging him not to touch the scars again.

"I would never harm you," Karris vowed.

Riena nodded, pulling her fisted hand to her lap when Karris released it.

"You must learn to touch others," he counseled her. "Mages you work closely with will expect you to touch them...and to allow them to touch you."

She hesitated for a moment, staring at her closed hand. It opened, and she turned around his body, until her robes brushed his back through his tunic.

Riena's hands feathered over his shoulders and back, tracing Karris's body. He bit back a groan at that.

"Did your master ever touch you?" he asked carefully.

"Not like this. Just the occasional touch on the cheek or forehead. My wrist, if he meant to instruct me."

Karris nodded. Jerin had most likely been afraid of Etan's wrath, mayhap even ordered not to introduce her to the power of touch. That possibility both angered and excited him. It wasn't Etan's right to deny Riena any of her training, but what education she lacked could now work to Karris's advantage. He untied the neck of his tunic, sighing as Riena hesitated.

"Touch my skin, Midman Romik." Karris managed to keep his voice even and free of emotion.

Her hands slid over the smooth skin of his chest and shoulders. Riena traced every muscle, then moved to his throat, following the smooth line of his jaw.

Karris's body throbbed in the power buzzing between them even in the light-blocking tent. "Do you feel it?" he whispered. "Do you feel how the power flows?"

"Yes, Caiben." Her voice was a mere whisper. Her hands continued their exploration, stroking at the length of his hair, then beneath. "Can Mages use this?" she asked.

He smiled at that, at the excuses she was giving herself to touch him again. "Yes. Touch before a channeling makes the body more sensitive, the power more pure." *But by the Mother, I have never touched another Mage like this.*

She nodded, her fingertips tracing his brow, the line of his nose, then his cheeks.

"Would you like to try it now?" he offered.

Riena touched the lower edge of his lips. "Yes. I would."

* * * *

Riena shook herself mentally. What madness was she playing at? Why had she agreed to this, when Caiben's touch was driving her mad? She winced in the realization that she'd agreed *because* Caiben's touch was driving her mad. Riena wanted this brand of madness with every drop of blood that circulated in her body.

Caiben strode to her, his chest peeking from the open front of his robes, his bare feet sinking deep into the grass beneath them. She shivered, averting her eyes so as not to let her longing show.

"Kneel with me," he instructed.

Riena nodded and did as he wished. He joined her, offering a tantalizing look at his chest to her downcast eyes. Caiben parted his robes further, a silent invitation to touch him again.

She pressed her palms to the planes of his chest, feeling the course of power intensely and immediately. Caiben laid his head back, soaking up more of Mother Moon's power and translating

166

it to the magic that shot up Riena's arms like liquid sunlight.

Riena closed her eyes, moving her hands over him without conscious plan. She hardly dared translate what she felt to the map of his body burned into her consciousness. The power intensified, stealing Riena's breath.

"That's right," Caiben rasped. His hands cupped her face, stroking over her cheekbones, tracing the outline of her lips. "Release the magic slowly. Help the plants grow."

She hadn't believed releasing their shared magic could feel more sublime than the buildup, but it did. Her nipples ached against their bindings, and her womb throbbed in time with the flow.

As if in answer, the pulse speeded. Riena imagined she could feel the throbbing in Caiben's body as well as her own. Her hand drifted to the soft expanse of his belly, over the waistband of his trousers, and Caiben shifted closer, his breathing harsh.

Riena forced her hand higher, reminding herself that she hadn't worked out how to approach a match with Caiben yet. She wasn't ready, wasn't prepared to demand the rights Mages' law allowed her and chance that he might accept such an offer.

Caiben stroked his thumb over her lips, then hesitated and repeated the action. Riena leaned forward on her knees, her fingers seeking out his lips blindly, stroking them. The heat of his breath on her sealing scars made her heart stutter, and

Caiben looked up in surprise, as if questioning her response.

Visions of Caiben's mouth closing over hers as Rosher's did on Lena's taunted Riena. She held his eyes, blowing her breath over his palms. His eyes closed in a look of ultimate pleasure, and Caiben leaned toward her, only at the last moment turning aside and pressing his lips less than a fingerwidth from hers.

Riena's body arched in the explosion of power. Her body mimicked that explosion, her climax rolling through her, as she released the magic abruptly. The grass shot up around them, shielding them from both the moon's light and prying eyes.

She drank in Caiben's shudder, falling with him into the grass. His muscles were clenched beneath her fingers, his male member hard against her hip.

Caiben opened his eyes, seemingly pained. His voice was hoarse and tremulous. "Well done, Romik. Are you well?"

Riena nodded, abruptly aware of the lines of Caiben's body imprinted on hers, his hands still stroking her face and neck, as if he thought to soothe her.

His hands retreated, and he placed a kiss to her forehead, as Master Jerin often did when she left him. "Go take your rest."

She nodded, caught between relief that she might escape undetected and a nagging sense of loss that he wasn't touching her. Riena headed for the tents on unsteady legs.

"Romik?" Caiben called after her.

Riena stilled. Had he felt the binding through the many layers she wore? Had he somehow gleaned what she was by the way she touched? It would almost be a joy to find he had. "Yes, Caiben?"

"You will accede to Mason at the Grand Rebirth," he informed her. "Study well."

Her heart sank that it was something so mundane. "Thank you."

Riena all but ran from his sight, taking *The Master's Words* to her pallet and praying Rosher wouldn't come to her smelling of sex with Lena again. She needed her wits about her, without such distractions.

There was so much to consider, so many possible ways to go about fighting for her freedom, that it made her head ache. There could be no chance of failure, no chance of Etan and Karris forcing her to what they wanted. Which was the right way? Which way would end well?

She considered her options. The Great houses were an uncertain thing. Their loyalty would war with their thirst for power, and Andrel and Etan were guaranteed to vote against her bid. That left seven Great houses in Voria, none of which she could count on to support her in a bid against King's Right.

The most attractive possibility had always been leaving Voria. By all accounts, King Tefan of Trelen was a staunch supporter of Mages' law. But would that change when the prize was so great? Would she find herself at the mercy of a worse king than Etan, when the day seemed won?

Either way, she had never exercised that possibility because of the chance of being captured trying to leave Voria. She had wanted to wait a year or two to attempt the crossing, but she couldn't do that if there was any chance of a life with Caiben.

Chapter Fifteen

Juno 10th, 4015

Karris glanced at Riena from the bar side, biting back a laugh. As good as she was at hiding her gender, in her most unguarded moments, she erred in execution. This was such a time.

Riena sat at the tavern table where they'd taken their mid meal, in peace, away from Rosher and Lena's play. *The Master's Words* lay open before her, and she moved back and forth between two of the sections of law, as if cross-referencing some point carefully.

In itself, that was innocent. Riena was often lost in the great book. It was her choice of position that announced what she was. One knee was crooked snug to the other, her higher foot swinging lightly. She hooked her hair behind her ear and leaned her chin onto the heel of one hand. All of this was unconscious, so intent was she on her reading.

His entire body ached to take her to some empty field and touch her again. Karris tried to tear his attention away, aware that he was staring at her intently in a public place, heedless of what these late-roaming night-sleepers would think of such a thing, believing them both male.

Dear Mother! Who could not know her for female?

As if in answer to his question, a man at another table ranged his gaze about and locked on Riena, taking in her position with a raised eyebrow and a smile of interest. Whether he knew

Riena for a female or thought her a male in search of male companionship, Karris had to end this encounter swiftly. The man took to his feet, and Karris ground his teeth in fury.

"Romik," he thundered.

Riena jumped to her feet, shooting him a questioning look.

"Bring the great book and accompany me." Karris threw a few coins on the bar, more than they owed, to be sure. There was no time to wait for an accurate accounting of their bill.

She brushed past the now-sour male without noting him or his mood. Karris watched long enough to be certain that her admirer wouldn't pursue her toward the doors, then turned and led the way outside. Her boots echoed on the wood walk outside, the only ones save his own, and Karris relaxed his guard.

He considered his options carefully. Karris didn't want Riena to endanger herself again, but how best to accomplish that? He buried a smile behind a stern face, a plan taking shape in his mind. Mayhap a reminder would be enough. "Do you prefer men?" Karris asked bluntly.

Riena stumbled, looking up to him with wild eyes. "Pardon?"

"Do you prefer men, Romik? Sexually? You certainly presented in the tavern as if you *did*."

She darkened. "It is not—"

"Acceptable to your position? I did not ask that. I asked if you preferred them."

"Of course not," she snapped, darkening further.

"All Mages are a bit feminine, Romik." He met her eyes, turning and advancing on Riena, following her retreat into a dark alley. "Some more than others. I see a good deal of uncertainty in you."

"Uncertainty?" she stammered.

"Yes. Most Mages wonder."

"Wonder?" Her gaze flicked to his mouth...then away, as if she answered her own question.

"What sex would be like with another male. If the feeling of his body would be more intense against your sensitive skin. But be warned that there are men you do not want to tempt with such an offer." Karris stepped toward her again, his body a hand width from hers as the wall stopped her retreat. "And those you might consider," he breathed.

Riena nodded shakily.

Karris touched her cheek. "There are many things that most Mages wonder, things much more tempting than even that." *Enough*, his mind argued. *You need to stop this.* But now Riena was so close he could smell her musk and feel her breath on his face.

"What things?" she whispered.

"How much more intense sex would be with another Mage, sensitive skin touching sensitive skin, the power building to release between them, climaxing together under the force of it. Do you wonder, Romik?" Karris wondered. His body came to aching attention to find out the answer to that question.

"You give me many new things to think about, Caiben," she answered carefully.

"Yes." *Think about it, Riena. Think about our bodies coming together in the light of Mother Moon.*

"Caiben?"

He placed his hands flat against the wooden wall on either side of her face, dropping his forehead to hers. "Yes, Romik?" His voice was gruff in his rising arousal.

"Do *you* wonder?"

"Never before," he answered honestly, "and never about a man who wasn't a Mage."

Riena nodded. "Neither have I."

"Do you now? With me?" *What do I do if she denies it?*

"Yes," she admitted in a breathless voice.

Karris groaned at that. He turned his face slowly, giving her every chance to refuse him. Some rational corner of his mind argued that she *should* refuse him. Darkness or not, they were in the center of town, both presenting the image of male Mages, about to explore something no *sane* male Mage would so close to other people.

Her lips brushed over his then retreated, returned, and lingered. The mead she'd had at mid meal made her lips sweet with fruit and honey. They were soft, softer than he remembered from his exploration of her in the shared channeling.

Riena sighed against his mouth, parting her lips slightly, innocent of what she offered him. Karris stroked the center of her upper lip with his tongue, dipping just inside her mouth and retreating again.

She opened eyes that were heavy in need, touching his lips with trembling fingers. Riena pulled her hand to her own lips, as if stunned that she'd allowed Karris leave to kiss her, that she'd done something so mad and impetuous, when her life and that of her brother depended on her disguise as a male.

"Romik?" he prodded, anxious to know her mind. Had he pushed too far?

"I must leave here," she whispered, seemingly in a daze.

His heart nearly stopped in terror. Why had he pushed so far? He hadn't had much to drink with their meal. Karris couldn't even blame his actions on that. "Nay. Stay with me. Complete your training...without payment. I will not attempt—"

"Caiben," she spoke over him. "I must leave Voria. I must leave *now*. To Trelen."

He stared at her in confusion. *Why now?* Why, when she'd not attempted to leave thus far and when it would be so simple to hide until the spring and leave in safety? "Leave Voria? But why?"

"I—cannot tell you. Not yet. Not..." She shifted *The Master's Words* against her chest with a furtive look around them, leaving the rest unsaid. What had she meant to say? Not here? Not now?

"What is it?" Where had this odd request come from and why just after he'd kissed her? Riena hadn't asked him to come along, but she hadn't acted as if she meant to go on alone, either.

Riena hesitated. "When— When King's law and Mages' law disagree, which is right?"

"Explain."

"I cannot," she repeated, her eyes pleading with him for a measure of trust. "Which would you support, Caiben? Tell me, please."

Karris considered their current situation, the kiss he'd just pressed for. Mages' law demanded a Mage reproduce if he was able to, which precluded more than a dalliance with another man. King's law left people to their own inclinations. Did Riena want his assurances that Karris wouldn't push to carry this encounter forward? That he wouldn't ask her to enter into a relationship that would reveal herself to him and place herself and her brother at greater potential risk?

Or was she addressing the larger issue with her question? Was she asking if he'd condemn her for fleeing justice? If he'd turn her over to Etan if given the chance? If so, she trusted him enough to bare her secret to him—but not here and now. Either way, his answer was the same.

"Mages' law," he assured her. "When I must choose, I support Mages' law."

Riena nodded, a shaky bob of her head that sent her hair flying about her overpale face. "I must leave Voria," she repeated. "I know the season is only half through but—"

"The Liomen Mountains are less than a week away." *They are close to the palace, but loosely guarded, because travelers rarely venture there.* There was little chance of being caught if they went that way. "We can be in Trelen in time for the Grand Rebirth."

"Then you will accompany me?" she asked hopefully.

Karris stroked her cheek, motioning her back to the walk. "I am your teacher, Romik."

She darkened at that, all but running from him into the light beyond the walls.

* * * *

Rosher stilled at the look on Riena's face. It was a look he'd not seen in months, something between nervous anticipation and misery. Riena had such a look in the final days before they ran, when the stress and terror of the price of failure had nearly driven her mad.

Was that it? Were they about to run again? If so, why? The possibility chilled Rosher. Why would they have to run now? If they did, he would have to leave Lena without even a word.

He closed his eyes, reining in his frustration. All his life, he'd deferred to Riena. He'd lost the love of his grandfather for her. He'd lost his mother's life to her. He'd lost home, safety, the food from his plate and clothing from his back, a sure future— And now, he was going to lose the woman he loved to her.

Rosher pushed that thought away. Riena had never wanted this life. She hadn't asked to be born or asked their mother to forego the midwife that might have saved her life. She hadn't asked Telan to hate her. Most of all, she hadn't asked to be a Mage, hunted by a king who knew no honor. Riena would tell Rosher to stay with Lena if she could.

Even that wasn't possible. If Riena were unmasked for what she was—or even if she ran and left Rosher behind, he would face Etan. Even if Lena could forsake her duty, her family would not, and there would be no way to hide who he was once they returned to the Great houses. Too many of her sister guards knew him well.

Rosher opened his eyes, steeling himself for the worst. "What is it?" he asked.

"We are leaving Voria and headed to Trelen. King Tefan is supportive of Mages' law. I have heard—"

Rosher winced. "And if he seeks to own you, as Etan and Karris do?" It was likely he would. Or were they going to hide in Trelen as they now did in Voria, hoping, day to day, not to be discovered for what they were?

Riena rolled her hands against each other, an exercise Master Jerin had taught her to acclimate her to the increased sensitivity. "I pray he will not be able."

"Why? How?" How could she be made unable to be mated? He prayed Riena didn't intend to have a midwife steal her fertility to ensure her freedom.

"When we reach the Lioman Mountains, I—" She turned away, pacing the length of the tent slowly. "I intend to tell Caiben everything, Rosher. I intend to offer myself to him as mate, just as Mages' law decrees I have the right to."

Rosher stared at her, struck mute in a mixture of terror and dismay. "He is loyal to Etan. He has a royal bodyguard," he reasoned. *A royal bodyguard of Andren's line who would love to see you dead or turned over.* "He will—"

Riena turned to him, shaking her head. "Nay. Caiben will not. I know he will not." But her eyes said that she wasn't certain about that.

"And if you are wrong about him?"

"What reason has he to hide what he is now? I know the true measure of the man, Rosher. If he is what I know him to be without any hope of more—" The tears spilled over, pinking her sensitive skin almost immediately.

"And...if you are *wrong* about him?" he repeated. Did she intend to run? To ask him to fight off Lena, for surely Rosher could never bend the royal bodyguard charged with a duty to his will.

"You will be safe in Trelen. I will bargain for that as I swore I would before we ran."

"And?" he prodded.

Riena took a calming breath, wiping away one track of tears. "If Caiben refuses me, I care not what happens to me," she admitted.

Rosher pulled her to his chest, closing his eyes to the faint smell of Caiben on her. Mages touched each other often. They were sensual creatures, and their skin was sensitized to touch by the power they channeled, all the more so after they sealed. Touching was important to them. Rosher prayed that Riena wasn't attributing more to Caiben's touches than the Master Mage intended.

"Are you certain?" he asked. If Caiben betrayed her, it would crush Riena.

She nodded.

"I brought you on this journey to ease your unhappiness. If Caiben is the source you seek to find peace, you must heed your heart."

"Thank you, Rosher."

He eased Riena to her pallet, holding her until she fell asleep in his arms.

His heart ached for what she was about to chance. If Caiben turned her over to Etan, Rosher wouldn't hesitate to seek his own death. He couldn't live on in the safety she offered while Riena accepted the king's blade—or the prince's unwelcome touch, uncaring and broken.

Rosher held her long after Riena slipped into that fitful sleep. He would meet death, but he wouldn't share that decision with Riena. Her happiness hinged on Caiben's choice. She would forsake her happiness to spare Rosher's life. That was not something he could allow.

Chapter Sixteen

Juno 16th, 4015

Riena closed the heavy winter robes over her body, thankful for the chill mountain air. Her hands shook in a sudden attack of nerves, and she fisted them in the Mason browns she was to be elevated to, again, tonight.

She'd come too far to turn back now, but Riena found herself much less certain than she had been six days earlier.

Caiben would come to take her to the meadow he knew of soon. They could watch the Silver Minute from the safety of the old-growth trees—or meet it together and be soulbound. As long as they met it as friends and not as foes, Riena would be happy to see the Grand Rebirth come. She shivered at the possibility of meeting the Silver Minute mated with Caiben.

Now that the moment was upon her, Riena found herself questioning her choice. Caiben hadn't been the same man since they'd begun their journey to the Lioman Mountains. He hadn't touched her since the kiss they'd shared, not even the touches he'd often offered in passing in the weeks before that night. Caiben had barely spoken to her since then, though he'd claimed her need to study for her ceremony.

Was he regretting that moment in the dark alley? Did Caiben believe her warped for her disregard of Mages' law on the subject of such a liaison? After all, Caiben had not the knowledge that she was anything but a male who had a deep interest in other men.

Riena sighed. One could drive herself mad arguing this. The only answer was to reveal the truth to Caiben and hope his anger at her deception—or his fear of or loyalty to Etan didn't overpower his moral code. Mayhap Caiben would be relieved to learn that he hadn't lusted after another male and would attribute his arousal to an inner sense that she was female.

"Romik," Caiben called. "It is time."

She took a deep breath and steeled herself for the challenge to come. Almost as an afterthought, Riena folded her arms over her unbound breasts to hide them from Caiben and Lena until she was prepared to reveal herself.

He turned and led her past Rosher and Lena, onto a soft, grassy incline that teased her bare feet with the whispers of power building around them. She glanced at Caiben. His feet were bare as well, though he wore light summer robes over a tunic and trousers, while she was nude beneath her own.

Riena shivered again at the thought of Caiben's nude body pressed to hers. It was an image that had plagued her dreams since the alley. She'd seen him stripped to the waist for channeling, only his braceband and trousers between them. Even before he'd kissed her, that had taunted her with the promise of things she had no right to hope for.

All Mages found the course of power sexually stimulating. When Riena sealed, she'd not had a name for the sensations that assaulted her. It hadn't taken her long to place a name to them.

The shared channeling was more sexually charged than a channeling undertaken alone, mayhap for the intimacy of the sharing. How many times had Riena glanced at Caiben's erect length in the moonlight, her nipples hard against the bands as he was against his trousers? Too many to count.

She startled as Caiben stopped in the meadow and turned to her. He crossed his arms over his chest, his expression stern but expectant.

"Now, Romik? Will you tell me why we had to leave Voria now?"

Riena swallowed a lump of pure fear. She had to do this. She couldn't live with herself if she didn't know whether or not Caiben could love her for herself.

* * * *

Karris looked to Riena. She stood, her feet apart and arms crossed over her chest, looking of grim determination and staunch fear at the same time.

"Romik?" he prompted her.

She nodded. "I asked you once if you favored King's law or Mages'."

"I remember." He remembered that moment well, terror as he never thought he'd feel in his life. Not knowing what had prompted her decision to leave Voria had stayed his hand these past few days. If he alienated her, he would never know what might have been.

"You truly do?"

"Of course." If his father had, they wouldn't be in this mess.

"Then if I told you I'd broken King's law—Etan's law, Voria's—in a way supported by Mages' law, would you drag me back and turn me over to King Etan? Or would you see me free to live my life here in Trelen?"

Karris's stomach clenched at that. *Free?* Had she discovered his identity? Whether she had or not, had she brought him here only to seek his permission to leave him and all of Voria for good?

"Caiben?" she asked.

He took to heart that she used his assumed name. If she knew him as Karris, would she use his true name now or wait until he'd given his answer?

"Caiben?"

He met her gaze. *She is not property. I cannot hold her unwilling; if I do, I am no better than my father.* "I would free you." His heart ached at the idea of letting her walk away. If he could turn his back on his place as prince, he would gladly guard her forever. "You have my vow that I would free you."

Riena sighed in relief, her shoulders relaxing. Her hands moved to the fasteners on her robes.

Karris watched her, barely breathing, anticipating her purpose. He should stop her. There was no reason to make Riena prove herself this way, but some selfish corner of his heart wanted to see her body, especially if she meant to leave him afterward.

She separated the robes to her navel, baring skin that seemed to glow in the rays of the disappearing moon. Riena bowed her head, pulling the robes from her shoulders and halting their slide at her hips with her sleeved arms. She trembled, waiting silently for his reaction, most likely fearing his condemnation.

"Riena." He breathed her name, rapt on her firm breasts, capped in a deep color that he would beg to see in the misty sunlight of high day or by a roaring fire simply to be certain of the exact hue. His member rose at the sight, begging to claim her.

Her eyes snapped up to meet his again, wide in terror. She seemed ready to bolt at the first move he made. "Will you turn me over to Etan and Karris?" she whispered.

Karris shook his head slowly. "We all have our secrets," he conceded. Would that he was lucky enough that she would be as understanding about his. "Why did you show me this? Why bring me here?"

Riena shifted from one foot to the other, no less frightened than she'd been a moment before, despite his calm acceptance and assurances. "*The M-Master's Words*," she stuttered.

"Go on."

"The Mages would let me—" She took a deep breath. "I would make you an outcast in Voria," she managed.

"An outcast?" His mind seemed incapable of following her logic.

"You have already broken King's law unknowing," she blurted. "You no doubt know that only Karris was to complete my training."

Karris raised an eyebrow at that, the urge to laugh aloud almost impossible to hide. He'd not broken the law, at all. True, he was the one his father decreed to teach her, but even were he not, Etan could hardly punish any Mage that had offered her training. No one outside the palace and her own instructors would know that she'd been denied training. Riena truly had no concept of how underhanded Etan had been in his quest to see her shackled to their house.

"I would have taken the punishment for it," she was quick to assure him. "I misled you."

"Then I would not have been an outcast," he noted.

She darkened.

"How would you make me an outcast, Riena? In my refusal to turn you over to Etan?"

"In letting me choose my mate, as *The Master's Words* decrees."

His heart hammered against his ribs. He dared not hope, but who else would Riena mean but himself? "What mate would you choose? If you were— You *are* free to choose now. What mate *do* you choose?"

Riena hesitated, the longing in her eyes like a being apart, hungry, unsated. "You."

Karris stared at her. This was more than he'd ever dared pray for. And yet...would she run from him when she knew the truth? "You want me as mate?"

She nodded, stiffening her spine as if preparing for his rejection.

"You do not know me." It would be dishonorable not to give her the chance to learn the truth. "My family, my worth, my—"

"I do not care," she interrupted him. "I know all I need to know."

"Do you?" What could she know? Riena didn't even know his true name.

"I do. I know your kindness and patience, your humor and intelligence. I know what the touch of your hands makes me feel."

Karris stepped toward her, stunned into silence.

"I am of no family, Caiben. Whether yours is high or low—"

"Your father was a Great Mage," he reminded her.

"His family has never acknowledged me."

"You could have any man you want. Even the prince—" He found himself a step closer with no memory of having moved the distance.

Riena raised her hand, stroking the line of his jaw. "I want *you*."

Karris nodded. "Nothing else matters to you? Nothing at all? Only the man you know as Caiben?"

"Nothing."

"Give me your vow."

"You will be my mate, chosen by Mages' law, joined soul to soul in the seal of power."

Karris smiled, cupping her head back in the cradle of his hands. "Soak up the dying rays of Mother Moon," he instructed.

Riena closed her eyes, and Karris stripped off his robes and tunic. Once she was bound to him, he'd end this madness. In truth, being soulbound would be his salvation. Surely, she would know he could never lie to her then.

Chapter Seventeen

Lena stilled, smiling at the sight of Karris and his young charge. Romik stood with his back to her, his head thrown back and his slight form unclothed to the waist.

She furrowed her brow at that. Lena had never seen Romik strip to the waist, though Karris did it often. Mayhap the boy was shy of his body in mixed company. He'd never taken a farmer's daughter to his bed, either.

She licked her lips at the sight of the narrow back he presented. Lena fully admitted to herself that she'd lost her heart to Gerry weeks ago, but there was something inherently sensual in the sight of a Mage at work, especially one that wasn't distantly related to her.

Her eyes moved to Karris, as he dropped his tunic atop his robes. *There must be a blight of some sort for him to willingly accept the Silver Minute uncovered this way, for both of them to do so.*

His hands settled on Romik's shoulders. "Have you attempted another Grand Rebirth since your first?" he asked.

"Nay. The pain—"

Lena winced at that. The Silver Minute had killed lesser Mages. Some chose never to seal, in fear that their magic wasn't strong enough to see them through. Karris had borne the burns for a week after his trial with the source of power, and his line was the strongest on Terra Set.

She replayed their words in confusion. Romik was young, much younger than Karris. When would he have had the opportunity to face a Silver Minute after his seal? No Mage sealed that young. Mayhap she had misheard them.

Her internal argument ended on a gasp at the sight of Karris. Her cousin brought his mouth down on Romik's, a tender kiss but not the kiss a man typically gave another man or even a child.

"Nay," she breathed, praying her observations were in error. There was nothing awkward in that kiss, nothing that seemed to indicate that this closeness between them was new and untried. "Nay," she repeated. She could not have missed something like this between them.

Lena prayed Romik would protest, that he would call a halt to Karris's mad behavior. The younger Mage did nothing of the sort. He met Karris's mouth with passion, firing her cousin's lust. Karris cupped Romik's buttocks and guided the Mason to his body. Their shared groan masked Lena's.

She frantically sought clarity. Was Karris truly mad? Or was he merely frustrated and alone? In need of the kinship he felt in Romik and confused?

Karris's mouth became more urgent, parting Romik's lips in a true lover's kiss. Lena grimaced at that. How long had they been coming together this way? How long, while she was lost in her own pursuits with Gerry? Etan would be likely to take her head for allowing this to happen.

Karris raised his head slightly, raining teasing kisses over Romik's mouth. He smiled. "Meet the Silver Minute joined with me."

"Nay," Lena repeated. *Mother Moon, how do I stop this?* If Karris did this, he would be bound to Romik for all time, his life tied to the young Mage, unwilling to survive long without Romik's presence in his life. Even if Karris took his destined mate—or any mate to provide heirs to the Vorian throne, it would be a hollow, unhappy experience for all three of them.

"Yes," Romik whispered.

Lena winced. Why couldn't the silly boy say no? *Because he has no concept who Karris is. I must end this. Surely, if Romik knows who Karris is, he will end this encounter. If he does not, I will have to end it for them.*

As if her thoughts were spoken aloud, Karris met Lena's eyes. His face hardened, promising death if she moved against him. His hand left Romik's body and motioned her away. Without waiting for her agreement, he cupped Romik's head in his hand and returned to his play.

Lena backed away, shaking her head. She had to end this before the Silver Minute. But how? Karris had warned her away, and he wouldn't hesitate to kill her for balking him directly in this. His madness was that complete, she could tell. Mayhap with help—

"Gerry," she breathed.

She looked to the moon, noting the time remaining until the Silver Minute. Romik's companion would end this if he knew the danger inherent to them all. If they didn't stop this

191

somehow, Etan would kill not only Romik but everyone who traveled with them, including his own son.

Nothing was more important than Karris's safety. She was sworn to protect him at all costs, even from himself...and even if it meant he'd slit her throat for it once the deed was accomplished.

* * * *

Riena opened her eyes as Caiben pulled the material from her arms. He paused, meeting her gaze as if to ask Riena's permission. She nodded, and he released her robes to the ground. Caiben's gaze roved over her body, hungry, hot in passion.

He cupped her breast in his palm. "What color are they?" he rasped.

She shook her head in confusion. He dipped his head, grasping the uncovered peak in his mouth. Riena threw her head back, running her fingers through his thick hair.

"Red-brown," she gasped, her mind locking on the information he sought.

Her senses swam. His mouth was hot, rough, then caressing, tugging lightly, inviting the energy coursing through her to his mouth, then to every fingerwidth of their bodies that touched. Her knees buckled. Caiben's arms tightened, then eased, lowering Riena to the bed of his robes thrown over the grass.

His hands explored her, making the flow of power between them surge. She moved her hand to his chest, watching the silver shine surrounding her fingers in awe.

Caiben shivered in response. "Know me," he instructed.

She grew bold, discovering the smooth skin and bands of muscle beneath the angles and hollows of his body. Riena lost herself in the mixed feeling of him and the glow that spread to encase them in its radiance, seemingly lighting the area as the moon dimmed.

Riena pulled at the buttons on his trousers, needing to feel Caiben inside her while the energy lasted. He obliged her, pushing his trousers away and settling over her, positioning the cradle of her body to accept him. His mouth captured hers again, waking her entire body to the hunger in him, her nerves bristling in a myriad of sensation, her own and his through the sharing. Riena shifted, inviting Caiben to make them one.

He cupped his hands beneath her thighs, his lips leaving hers. "Be sure."

She nodded again. "I want you."

Caiben thrust deep inside her, stilling as if awash in the same sensations coursing through her. Riena's body was pleasure and pain, chill air and hot tendrils of mixed breath, the solid reality of flesh on flesh in the intangible vortex of light massaging her, inside and out.

He moved slightly, rocking his hips back and forth, the friction of their bodies and the rising heat pushing her to the edges of endurance.

"Caiben," she pleaded. "I have to."

"Nay. Do not release the magic. Not yet." He raised his head. "The moon is dying. Trust in me."

The moon went black. The world was still, waiting, abruptly cold.

Caiben's pace sped, his body's movements fierce and smooth as a royal bodyguard's attack. He cursed, his grip on her legs tightening. She grasped at his hips, teetering at the edge of the vortex.

"Not yet," he begged—or perhaps he pleaded with her. That much was uncertain.

The first sliver of the Mother Moon reappeared, and Riena pulled Caiben hard inside her. "Forever," she wished.

"Love me," Caiben shouted over her.

Then the Silver Minute was upon them. Riena's body tingled in the first fingers of light, tightening in the rising heat. Caiben's eyes half-closed in pleasure.

"Burn," she moaned, knowing the intense heat was only a heartbeat away.

"Accept it," Caiben soothed her.

Riena held his eyes as the Minute crested, the silver light dancing like flames over their skin. It filled her as Caiben did, his heat touching the last of her and making her his. She screamed in pleasure at that. If there was pain, Riena didn't note it.

"Now," Caiben breathed. "Direct it."

She fought for clarity, unwilling to release such a wave undirected. Panic set in as her mind failed to grasp at a purpose.

"Anything," he shouted. "Anything you wish, but do it now."

It has to be now. The shared energy was bottled, but their souls were not bound until it was released, their essences joined by the Mother's Grand Rebirth, so powerful that even a non-Mage mate could be soulbound at this precious moment. If it wasn't while the Silver Minute shone, they might be destroyed in the joining.

Riena let the magic flow into the ground around them, vaguely noting her goal. Caiben uttered an oath on the Mother, watching the changes with wide eyes. The ground shook and cracked. Shadows fell, and the growth overtook them, and still the energy coursed from Caiben, through her, and into the rapid growth around them.

Caiben shielded her with his body, his breathing harsh in her ear. Then the power abated. Riena looked at the forest of thick bushes around them in a weary sort of understanding.

"Blue Ladies." Caiben laughed, a nervous little sound.

She closed her eyes, nodding her agreement. Why she chose Blue Ladies was a mystery to her. Mayhap because she found their petals so soothing. Their scent made her head swim again, her tender body aching in renewed hunger, though Riena was certain she was too tired to contemplate such a thing.

His lips touched her forehead. "Rest, Riena."

"I do love you," she whispered.

"And I you—forever."

* * * *

Rosher looked up in surprise as Lena bolted from the trees. Her eyes were wild and her face pale. He rose to meet her, his heart sinking at her state of panic.

"Gerry," she gasped, dragging at his arm as if to pull him after her. "I need your help."

"What is it?"

"Romik and C—C—" She shook her head, panting for breaths and looking shaken or dizzy.

He grumbled a curse. Had Riena been wrong about Caiben, after all? Was he enraged at her deception, at his unwitting part in it? "Are they dueling?" he asked weakly, allowing her to pull him along.

Why had she come to him for help? Lena was a royal bodyguard. She would protect Caiben at any costs, and if she and Caiben stood against them, Riena and Rosher would be delivered to Etan as quickly as horses could cover the distance.

Lena shook her head. "Nay. They— They mean to meet the Silver Minute and soulbind." She darkened at that.

Rosher bit back a laugh of relief, stopping at the fireside. "Thank the Mother!"

"Nay," she shouted. "You do not comprehend the problem."

"We are outside the borders of Voria," he began.

"Outside or inside, Karris is prince," she thundered.

"You told me your duty to Caiben surpasses all others," he noted, furious with her for her inconstancy. Either Caiben was most important, or her duty to return Riena to Etan and Karris was. It could not be both.

"Have you any concept of what Etan will do?" she reasoned.

"We are outside the borders of Voria. We are safe from Etan here."

She growled in frustration. "*Nowhere* is safe from Etan; not if they do this. That is why I have to stop him."

"To make them miserable?" Rosher shouted. "I thought you said your duty—"

"I do not understand you. I stand here telling you that Karris is about to soulbind himself to your master, and you *approve*? The Vorian Heir is—"

"Wait," he asked, his head spinning. "Caiben is Prince Karris?"

Lena threw up her hands in a show of frustration. "Did I not say that?"

Rosher looked to the forest in growing unease. "Nay. You did not."

"Then you will help me end this?" she asked hopefully.

"Was...was Romik willing to mate?" Mayhap this would be for the best. Mayhap—

She gaped at him. "What?"

"Willing? Eager? Was—was Romik *eager* to soulbind?" Soulbound, Karris would be unable to cause Riena pain, lest he feel it too. Soulbound, there would be no secrets between them. Surely, Karris would not enter into that state in anger or subterfuge. The price of it would be too high. They would both be destroyed in the joining.

"Yes," she whispered miserably. "Now, *please* help me stop them. The moon is nearly gone." She started to back away.

Rosher grasped her arms, shaking his head. "Nay. If you have any mercy, let them bind."

"Mercy? For your master? He has no concept what is at stake here," she choked.

"But Karris does, and it is *he* you must show mercy for tonight."

"Your master—"

"My sister."

Lena stilled. She shook her head, her brow creased.

"If Karris has stayed this long and never told you who Riena is, his motives are pure. He could have had her at any time, but he showed her patience and caring. He showed her respect, which is something she'd never dared pray for from him. Please— Let them bind."

"She does not know," she whispered, looking to the trees.

"Riena loves him enough as Caiben to offer herself, to bind her soul to him. Do you believe she will not welcome an end to our running?"

Lena seemed unconvinced.

Rosher led her toward the fire. "Let them bind. In the meantime, warm with me."

Her confusion was replaced with a familiar hunger. "Now that I know Romik is actually a woman—"

He drew Lena to his body. "Their loveplay excited you?" he growled.

She kissed at the curls peeking through the open neck to his tunic. "Would that disturb you?" she teased.

"You *always* disturb me." The night fell dark around them.

"The mighty Rosher of Bentin is disturbed?" she asked with a raised eyebrow. "The guard crusher? The—"

He felt his cheeks burn and stilled her outburst with a kiss. "Taunt me much more and I will spend the rest of the night disturbing *you*," he warned.

"And half the day?" she requested on a sigh.

The Silver Minute raced toward them. "Be my mate," Rosher shouted to the Grand Rebirth.

"Yes," Lena's shout followed his.

Silver light bathed them in its blinding glow. From far away, cries echoed, then fell silent. Rosher smiled in the knowledge that he and Riena had both gotten the wish they wanted most.

Then the ground began to quake lightly beneath their feet. Rosher shot a startled look at Lena and pulled her into the forest. She led the way up the mountainside to a break in the trees.

"Dear Mother," she breathed, ranging her gaze up the flower bushes that dwarfed the tallest old-growth on the mountain.

"Where do we start?" Rosher asked helplessly.

The question was answered for him. The thorn stalks parted, and Karris stepped from within, bare-chested, Riena—hastily covered in a tunic and torn robes—in his arms.

"Karris, is she well?" Rosher asked.

Karris smiled. "She is better than well, Brother. Riena is merely fatigued."

He sighed in relief, gathering Lena to his side. "I trust Lena may share my tent this day?" he asked pointedly.

"I would stand for nothing less."

Chapter Eighteen

Juno 17th, 4015

Karris groaned at the hands caressing his chest. Mother Moon, waking with Riena was better than any dream he'd had of it.

"Caiben," she called playfully.

He sighed. That was the first duty of the moonrise. The next time he took Riena, she'd scream his true name in the heat of passion.

"Ah, Riena." He ran his hands through her hair, hair that she'd cut shorter than his own in her bid for escape. He would know its weight on his chest in years to come. He'd heard it from reliable sources that Riena had always prided herself in her hair.

"My husband wakes." Her hand traveled down his stomach as it often had before she had the freedom to do what she likely planned now. "And aroused by my touch," she teased.

He stilled her before she could circle his ready length. Karris absolutely would not take Riena again before this madness was ended, once and for all, despite what a tempting star spirit she was. "Not yet."

She tensed, all but invisible in the light-blocking tent, since the moon had not fully risen. "What is it?"

"Why did you run?" he asked. Karris was fairly certain he knew her reasons, but addressing them openly would be best—now, before he revealed himself to her.

Her lips brushed his shoulder. "Does it matter?"

"I wish to know."

He traced her nipple, attempting to put her at ease with him again. Riena arched to his touch, and the tip came to a hard point against his sensitive palm. Karris laid a kiss on the other one softly.

Red-brown. She said they were red-brown. I must investigate that.

"Fear," she whispered.

"Fear? Of Prince Karris? Or of the king?"

She hesitated.

Karris reached over her and lit a lamp to see her better. Riena was expressive. Her eyes would tell him much more than her words would. "Of Karris?" he repeated.

He glanced to her breasts, unable to deny himself the treat. *Mother Moon, the color is stunning.*

"In part. I met him only once."

"Go on." He guided Riena to his body, pressing her cheek to his chest.

Her fingers stroked at his cheek. "We were children when Etan claimed me for his son in King's Right."

"And Karris?"

"He hated me. He never wanted me as his mate. The look he gave me when Etan ordered him..." She shook her head in apparent misery.

Karris kissed her forehead, closing his eyes to the memories of his fury. He'd refused to see her for the rest of her stay, taken meals in his rooms, and turned from her the few times their paths had crossed in the corridors. Karris's behavior had been deplorable. He'd been a willful child, taking out his anger on the wrong target.

Had it really haunted her all these years? Yes, it had. He could feel the stirrings of her upset, even now. "I cannot blame you for fleeing him."

Riena sighed, her breath teasing at his chest. "I did not truly know him," she noted. "That was all I knew of him, and that was a decade ago."

She admitted that? Riena admitted that it wasn't simply belief that he couldn't have changed much that drove her. "Then why choose this course?"

"If you were told you had to mate with someone you had not chosen, would you have submitted quietly? Taken her to your bed without any thought of your own happiness?"

"Nay. I would not." He hadn't. Once Karris had reasoned that Riena was not the cause of his plight, he'd made his father pay years of discomfort for his decision to shackle Karris to Riena unwilling.

She smiled, nipping at his chest. "Tell me the story of yourself."

"You know all you need to know," he reminded her, a smile pulling up at his lips at that, his heart pounding that the time had come to reveal himself and risk his heart.

Already, the agony of their joining threatened him. Though there was only one way to escape him now, it was a way that would kill them both. Being soulbound was a precious thing. Mayhap Karris had been wrong to allow this, after all. If she could not accept him, it would mean disaster.

Riena turned over him, fitting her body to the planes of his. "I have shared all my secrets with you. I would know my husband. Why would you fear that?"

So, she feels my fear. That could be an advantageous thing. If Riena thought to use their link, she would know his heart was true.

Karris nodded. "What would you know?"

"Everything. I could never ask you anything." She blushed, laying her head on her folded hands and waiting for him to tell her the story of himself.

"Because I might ask in return, if you did?" he guessed.

She nodded.

"Ask me anything," he promised. That way, they might talk a while before she asked anything that would reveal his identity beyond a shadow of a doubt. Nay. She would ask something basic first: his family, his past—

Riena raised his hand to her mouth, tracing her lips over his sealing scars. Karris groaned, his body aching for hers that simply.

"Why do you wear this braceband?" she asked. "Even now, you wear it."

Karris sobered. "Because, I am scarred."

Her eyes widened. "May I see?"

He nodded, forcing shallow breaths as she unlaced the leather. Riena turned his hand to see the marks better in the lamplight. She kissed the longest—the one that had pricked the artery and ripped when he jerked away, tearing and causing almost all of the blood he'd lost that night.

"How did this happen?" she asked, seemingly fascinated. "Tell me the tale."

Karris stroked her cheek. "It was a duel. I was very young and foolish. I challenged another Mage, believing in my arrogance that my opponent could not possibly be stronger than I was."

"He was?"

"That Mage was possibly the strongest I have ever met," he vowed.

"Etan," she breathed. A slight edge of fear swirled between them.

Karris chuckled to put her at ease. "Nay, though I have indeed met the king."

"Karris then." She winced at that, mayhap at the idea that Karris had scarred him like this. Was she imagining harsh treatment for herself at her intended's hands had she not run?

"Nay. Stronger even than Karris, in many ways."

"What Mage is stronger," she began in awe. Riena gasped, looking to his wrist fearfully. "Nay," she whispered. Shock seemed to eclipse all else, save a niggling of unease.

Karris reached for her hand, tracing the scar on her thumb he'd left, wishing he could take it away as he had many times since that night. He offered a weak smile. "You know all you need to know, Riena. Who am I?"

"Karris." She eased away from him, suddenly wary, covering her breasts with the tunic he'd taken from her sleeping body when they'd reached his pallet.

He watched the growing distance between them in dismay. "Does my name change anything? I am the same man I was last night, save two differences."

"What differences?" Riena halted her retreat at the edge of his pallet. Her voice shook in a mixture of fear and anger, and tears welled in her eyes.

"You chose to give yourself to me. You are not mine because you were ordered to be mine. You came to me and asked me to be your mate, just as Mages' law allowed you to do."

"And if I had chosen another?"

"I vowed to free you, no matter your choice," he reminded her gently. "My father would have flayed me alive for it, but I gave my vow."

"How long have you known?"

Her breathing was ragged, and she looked to the flap as if fearing for Rosher's safety. Yes, her fear tainted the flow between them, a sour feeling in the pit of Karris's stomach. Riena's hand fisted, a momentary panic taking hold. She released it almost immediately, no doubt reasoning that she would only injure herself in the attempt to escape him physi- cally. Uncertainty ran riot in her.

Karris sighed at that. "He is safe, Riena. I am not my father."

Hope rose up in her and was swallowed by her unease. Was it really so difficult for her to accept his sincerity?

You have spent all this time lying to her, he reminded himself. "I speak the truth, Riena. You must feel that. Use the flow between us. You have my vow that I mean neither of you harm. I never have."

Riena's hand fluttered to her heart. Karris held his breath, praying that she felt it, that she knew his words were true. Her breathing hitched, and her emotions calmed slightly.

She nodded, meeting his eyes again. "How long?"

"When the rogue Mages attacked you."

"Why did you complete my training? Why did you not confront me? Why did you bring me out of Voria? Why did you give your vow to free me? Why—" Her words tumbled over each other, a torrent of confusion crashing through the floodgates of her mind.

"Shhh," he soothed her. "I favor Mages' law, remember? You were never my father's to *give*. It was not his right to claim you for me. It was not his right to deny you training." He stroked her hand, taking heart in that she didn't push him away. "I could not leave you," he admitted.

"You were angry that I ran from you." Riena didn't question it. Her emotions were less riotous, more ordered, as if she were reasoning herself to some end.

Karris sighed, knowing that she would know all the truths of him. He could not lie about his anger any more than he could lie about the things he wanted her to know. "At first. You never gave me a chance. I wanted to put you at ease with me. I wanted to know you before the mating night arrived...and to let you know me. I asked, Riena. Over and over, I asked, but by the laws of King's Right, I could not go to you before the mating night—to your bed or even to see you, unless you invited me there."

She nodded, dropping her gaze. Her emotions were a tangled skein of embarrassment and understanding. She didn't question his words. Riena couldn't question them in light of what she felt from him. How could she? He'd spoken the truth.

He continued, needing her to know the truth of his intentions. "More than that, I suspected why you ran. I had no right to take you back, without your consent."

"You did," she grumbled. A bitter bite at the thought of it coursed over their link.

Karris raised her hand, drawing Riena toward him slightly to kiss her knuckles. "Nay. I did not."

She looked to her hand, the hope stronger now.

Karris turned her hand, blowing a puff of air over her sealing scars. Her eyes closed in pleasure, and her arousal sang over his nerves.

"Can you doubt me, Riena? Can you deny what my soul tells you?"

"No." There was no bitterness in her at that. Despite whatever misgivings she had about the situation, she craved him still.

Karris brushed his lips over her sealing scars, drinking in her groan of pleasure.

Riena eased toward him, leaning over his body, the tunic laying forgotten in her lap. She laid her forehead to his, her breath tickling his lips. "Tell me you love me again," she requested.

He smiled, knowing her intentions in that. "I love you," he replied.

Her reaction to that was fierce and immediate. Happiness warred with hope, relief, and even lust. The effect was overwhelming. Karris turned his face as he had in the dark alley, finding her lips and enticing Riena to lose herself in their shared passion.

"You need never run again," he promised. "You have my vow that all will be well."

She nodded, meeting his lips again, her acceptance of the future peace apparent in both her fervor and their link.

Karris tangled his fingers in her hair, letting himself sink into the call of their mating. *Soulbound.* There was nothing more pure and perfect in all the world.

Riena startled at the sound of approaching mounts, pushing herself to sitting again and bringing the tunic back to her chest. The sharp feeling of dismay and betrayal burned in her as tears burned at her eyes, threatening to fall.

"The other difference," he assured her.

She met his eyes, questioning silently.

"You have broken no laws."

"I *ran* from you," she protested.

Karris smiled, pulling on his trousers and dragging the star blue sash from the bottom of his pack, belting it snug around his waist. He handed off the pack of Riena's belongings he'd carried for almost a season to her.

"You ran *to* me," he corrected her. "Trust in me as you did at the Silver Minute."

His heart ached at that. Even if he could have hidden it, Karris wouldn't have. Her trust in him was imperative. Without it, there was no hope of making this right. Only together were they strong enough to demand the rights due Riena.

She nodded, placing her fate in his hands.

Karris pulled back the flap, blinking his eyes in the glare of the rising moon, still powerful from her rebirth. There were only two riders inside the perimeter of the camp: Etan and Reesa. He could make out the vague outlines of the others in the trees, ready to attack at a motion from either of the two he faced.

His father stared down from atop his horse, his face grim.

Karris nodded. He'd known when Riena's release of magic had been so explosive that Etan would track them. No doubt, Tefan would arrive in another day, but the Vorian palace was much closer to the border than the Trelen. They were too close to either for their soulbind to go unnoticed.

"Explain this," Etan demanded. "The forest of thorns. The tremors. The local people are terrified. They believe Mother Moon is angry with them. Why would you do such a thing?"

Lena launched from the second tent, her tunic rumpled and looking decidedly tussled and thoroughly loved. Her state didn't escape Etan's notice. His jaw tightened in the promise of punishment for dereliction of duty.

Etan's gaze moved back to Karris. "And explain two months with no word to me."

"I have spent the two months undoing your errors," Karris snapped. *Your crimes.* He motioned his father for a moment of silence. "I have traveled in the company of my mate."

Etan darkened, but his questions remained locked inside him. Karris glared at him. If his father wished to know the answers to those questions, he would have to ask them in a civil tone. It was a game his father had played with Karris many times during those years when Karris sought to punish Etan for his pending mating. Now it was Karris's turn to play the master.

"Who is this mate?" Etan asked carefully.

"The only woman I will ever love. She agreed to be soulbound with me, willingly and with no knowledge of who I am."

Etan's hands fisted on his reins, a move that must have driven spikes of pain from his scars to his shoulders. "You taunt me," he growled.

"A wise king once told me that a Mage should be trained well enough to ignore taunts," he countered.

"A wise *prince* should know better than to taunt a king."

Karris chuckled. "I will be certain to remember that."

"And still you taunt me."

"Not at all, Father."

"Then answer me."

Karris raised an eyebrow, waiting for his question, giving Etan a taste of his frustration over the last two months.

"Karris," he shouted.

Riena's unease turned to outright fear, and Karris willed her to feel his calm, to know that he would allow her to come to no harm, only marginally aware of his father's demand.

His voice was slow and measured. "Yes, Father?"

"The woman's name," he ordered.

He sighed, shaking his head. "You will not ask, will you?" Karris didn't wait for an answer, turning and peeking inside the flap to make certain that Riena was dressed.

She was terrified, her hands fisted in the silk of her mating robes. Karris smiled in encouragement. Dear Mother, but she was beautiful. Much more beautiful than he'd imagined she'd be when he'd commissioned the robes for her.

Karris offered his hand. She took it, trembling, stepping out behind the shelter of his shoulder with her head bowed, so she wouldn't have to meet Etan's fury head on.

Etan blew out his breath, most likely in relief. "Well done, Karris."

"I know why you did this," Karris informed him, turning Riena into his arms. "I know you feared Riena would bind herself to another, and that Mage would be strong enough to take the throne."

Etan darkened. He didn't deny the charges Karris levied against him, but he didn't offer comment either.

"You were wise to worry, Father." Karris brushed his lips over hers, letting the threat sink in before he spoke again. "You broke laws to bring Riena to me. You even used an illegal aphrodisiac on my gifts to her to sway Riena to my bed."

She gasped in surprise, pulling a fold of the mating robes to her face and shooting Etan a look of pure fury.

Karris touched her face, soothing her without words. Etan's treachery would not go unpunished.

From the corner of his eye, Karris saw Lena and Rosher closing on their position, ready to defend them if Etan and Reesa moved. Their foes took note of the action but made no move against them. Karris hadn't stated his intention to take the throne by force. There was no treason to fight—yet.

"And yet you failed," Karris informed his father.

"But you took her as mate," Etan began in a growl.

"Nay, Father. Riena took *me*, just as Mages' law allows, as she should have been allowed from the first."

"Either way—"

"She is mine. If you ever come between us again, your worst fears will be realized."

"You threaten me?" Etan asked, his face as misty white as the midday sun.

Riena grasped at his wrist—lightly so as not to cause herself pain, her fear a living thing. Karris drew the hand to his heart, smiling as her terror receded.

"I give you fair warning. If the king acts dishonorably, he does not deserve his throne. You taught me that. With Riena at my side, I have the power to right many wrongs. Not even you will stand against us. My household is my own, and I will balk no interference to that."

Karris jerked his head at their bodyguards meaningfully. That meaning wouldn't be lost on either Reesa or Etan. Any move against Rosher or Lena would be seen as a move against Riena and Karris.

Etan nodded, his jaw tight in fury.

"Then leave us." Karris lifted Riena into his arms and turned into their tent. He would finish what Riena started that moonrise, whether his father sat outside to listen or not. Karris followed her down onto his pallet with a groan of need.

She looked to the flap nervously. "Was that wise?" she whispered. "Turning your back on him after that threat?"

"Yes. It is."

He'd shown no fear, been confident in their abilities together. Etan didn't dare test it, not after they'd scarred the face of Terra Set with their soulbind.

He eased the hooks on her silk robes from their loops expertly, anxious to hear her cry his name, his true name.

Her nipples puckered against the silk, and she arched to his body. "Karris," she called in a low voice.

He chuckled at her breathless whisper.

"He has not departed yet," she noted.

"Good. We can give him something more to worry about."

Riena licked her lip, as he pulled her robes aside to bare her fully. "What did you have in mind?"

"*The Master's Words* says a female Star Mage conceived at the Silver Minute—"

Karris made it no further. Riena pulled his mouth to hers, her hand clasped to the back of his neck, her chest hitching in laughter even as she met him passionately.

"And if we did not succeed?" she asked archly.

"There will be another Silver Minute every five years."

Riena's laughter sang over his nerves.

Karris stroked her cheek. "I know a circle of flowers that has not known such happiness in far too long. Would you meet the Silver Minute with me there?"

She nodded, using the motion to brush her lips over his sealing scars. He closed his eyes to the feeling of her fingers peeling away his trousers. Riena urged him toward her by a grip on his sash. It was irreverent, and yet Karris smiled at how appropriate the move was.

He thrust deep into her, crying out as she forced her body to his. The energy between them spiked even in the near darkness of the tent, rising as their bodies came together, time and again.

As if she had taken Karris's plan to make his father nervous to heart, Riena was unrestrained in her vocalizations. She moaned and panted, urging Karris on with pleas for more. When their climax crashed over them, she made his wish reality and screamed out his name.

Karris furrowed his brow at the release of power. It was much more intense than their lovemaking had generated, no doubt drawing on Riena's personal reserves a bit.

"What did you—"

She chuckled at Etan's muttered curses.

"What did you do?" He repeated, needing to know what mischief she'd wrought.

Riena smiled a wholly feminine smile as she moved against him. "I gave him something more to worry about," she teased.

Karris raised an eyebrow in surprise. "For instance?"

"I simply transfigured that ugly little bush into something more beautiful," she answered a little too innocently.

He grinned. "Would they be Blue Ladies?" he asked.

Riena shook her head slowly. "No. I thought I would offer him a more thought-provoking gift."

Karris furrowed his brow in confusion.

She pulled his head down, nestling her lips close to his ear. "Pink Daughters," she whispered.

He laughed in spite of himself, picturing Etan's reaction in startling detail.

Riena reached back and raised the hood of her mating robe around her face, drawing in a deep breath. Her eyes glittered in the sexual excitement that coursed through their link to Karris. He looked to the robe in understanding. She was using the Blue Lady nectar on them both.

"What are you planning?" he asked suspiciously.

"How will he know if it was the Silver Minute?" she hinted.

Karris nodded, visions of their future together dancing in his mind.

The End

The Master's Lover

Star Mages #2

Brenna Lyons

Dedicated To...

Werekitten, Little Tamer, and Implet- my own little Oranas.

Thus, it begins...

Mey 12th, 3055

Galon glanced around the barroom, his heart pounding in anticipation. It was always like this when he sought out a sexual partner, and it had been far too long since he'd had the opportunity to do so. Though he knew of no other mages in the area, and King's law allowed a mage male lovers, he'd taken blows more than once—by mage and farmer alike—for his inclinations.

He'd never dared report the abuse; his attackers knew he wouldn't. Though King's law allowed Galon his sexual choices and forbid such abuses, Mages' law was against him. Complaining would only invite more of the same.

A rough farmer caught his eye. The man was the type he most often succeeded with. Whether they honestly preferred men on their sheets or simply wanted to experiment wasn't Galon's concern. Even if they wanted the thrill of topping a mage and nothing more, they were both getting what they wanted from the liaison.

He looked around at the thinning crowd of night sleepers, thankful that the seat he'd chosen afforded none but the farmer an unobstructed view of him. It was time to take a chance.

Galon met the farmer's gaze and crossed one leg over the other, fitting the upper knee onto the curve of the lower. It was a well-known sign among men, less so among women, who also chose to sit this way at times. Any man observing the move would know his mind and meaning by it.

The farmer hesitated, then smiled, his gaze ranging the length of Galon's body, from the top of his midman-green hood to his scuffed boots, the same boots he'd worn on the day of his escape, more than a year earlier.

He forced the memories of the frightened nineteen-year-old he'd been from his mind. Galon had learned a lot about staying alive in the past year, more than he'd thought he still needed to learn when he'd left home.

But now was not the time for those thoughts. He waited for the farmer's determination, hardly daring to breathe.

A nod of his blond head, a single terse movement, had Galon releasing a breath he hadn't realized he'd been holding. The farmer tossed a few coins on the bar and rose, striding through the door and into the street.

Galon knew what to expect next. The ritual of a mage finding a male partner was always roughly the same.

Unless it is a trap.

He pushed that thought away, tossed a silver coin on the table to pay for his half-finished ale, and strolled out as if he had nowhere to be in particular. Behind his robes and trousers, his cock was already half-erect and aching, his heart racing. He forced his breathing to a slow, steady stream. Mother, but it had been far too long since he'd touched another.

As he'd expected, the farmer was just turning the corner into an alleyway, the one between the granary and a storehouse. He was leading the way for Galon. If the farmer had tarried and waited for

Galon to rise first, it would be a sign that Galon would choose the place for their play. But the farmer had risen first; the choice of where was his and not Galon's.

He gave the farmer a lead of a few moments, playing the game though he practically salivated to get to the end of said protective misdirections as quickly as possible. Galon walked faster than he should, that thought driving him on.

In fact, Galon was so intent on his goal, the knife was at his throat before he realized the farmer wasn't at the far end of the alleyway, waiting for a sound to turn another corner.

"Your money, young mage," his captor growled.

Galon bit back a groan at that. He'd been beaten several times; it was a sad risk he took. But no one had robbed him as part of the punishment before.

He reached into his robes, sick at the thought of losing what he'd amassed. With only half the season left to work and his savings gone, his winter would be very lean indeed.

Mayhap leaner than my first.

The farmer grasped the pouch in his free hand, chuckling darkly. "It never fails that your type do what I order."

Galon ground his teeth at that. It was galling to know himself for one of the most powerful beings on the planet yet, by a twist of the Mother's humor, find himself powerless before his lesser.

"You will move on to your amusements without a word. Will you not, Mage?"

"Of—of course," he stammered. With a knife at his throat, what else would Galon say to such a command?

There was a jingle of coins cut short, no doubt the farmer stuffing them into a pocket. Then the hand that had held his pouch moments before crossed Galon's body and cupped his cock.

He thanked the Mother that it was flaccid. *Better the chance he will leave without doing me physical harm.*

It wasn't that Galon feared a beating. Between his father and those he'd met on his travels, he'd learned to take a beating well. One always healed, unless he were killed in the attack, and then his troubles were over.

But bruises on a Star Mage were not easily explained away. There were only so many times one could claim a fall or other accident without people whispering things he didn't want whispered to other mages.

The knife left his throat, and the hand at his cock started stroking. Galon closed his eyes, trying to stifle his natural reaction to such a masterful and knowing touch.

That was impossible. The farmer had obviously played at men before, and it had been far too long since anyone had played at Galon. He hardened, his face burning at the reaction even as he prayed the farmer was going to follow it out. It would almost be worth the loss of coin to find relief from this maddening arousal.

"You are a responsive little whore," the farmer grumbled.

So that is the game he likes to play. Galon had played it and many others. Long ago, he'd resigned himself to the fact that there was seldom pleasure without pain, seldom satisfaction without some cost to his self-respect in bargain.

The farmer's hand delved through the split in Galon's robes, wrenching the lower fasteners open, returning to play at his body. Galon bit his lip, swallowing a groan of pleasure. Mother, but he wanted this.

No, not this, but this will do.

He'd had worse, men who were curious but wanted to pretend they weren't, men who were fast and hard, beating him harshly when they had spent...or when he had. At least this farmer had played in a man's body before.

Even if the farmer liked a rough fuck, chances were that Galon could get some satisfaction out of it. The fact that he was bothering to work Galon up was proof enough of that.

"Beg me for it. Beg me to take your ass."

The words stuck in Galon's throat, and his jaw tightened involuntarily, holding back what the farmer had ordered. Even if he wished to speak the words—*and I don't*—they wouldn't emerge. It was the one thing he'd vowed he'd never do again.

With a sinking sensation in his gut, Galon forced his mouth and lungs to form his answer. "No." He winced at the note of decision in his voice, knowing the retaliation would be swift and painful.

The hand left his cock and the farmer backed off a step. Galon's dash for freedom lasted only a step. A hand closed around the back of his neck, and the farmer turned and propelled him into the stone granary wall with a considerable amount of force.

Light danced before his eyes, and the metallic taste of blood flooded his mouth. Galon pushed weakly at the stone, disoriented, cursing the fact that they were in town. Illegal or not, he would have used his powers against the farmer were they in a place to do so...a forest or even a field of crops. His attacker had planned this well.

Liar, his mind shouted at him. He wouldn't retaliate, because he couldn't risk being judged for his sexual tastes, and they both knew it was true.

The crush of the farmer's body was abruptly gone, and Galon's knees buckled. The stone scraped at his face, and the force of his landing on the dirt track drove the air from his lungs.

He fought his way up from the brink of unconsciousness, his blood running cold at the sight of a Master Mage crouching over him. The red piping of a Great House stood out in stark contrast to the black robes in the light spilling from the street.

"What crimes?" the master barked.

"Stealing," Galon replied weakly, uncertain of how much the master saw of their interaction. *With any luck, he hasn't seen more than the farmer's attack on my person.* "And assault."

The master's gaze slid from Galon's face to the open front to his robes. His fingertips feathered over Galon's aching cock, sending a wave of delight through his body.

It was gone nearly as quickly as it settled on him, about as quickly as it took the master's jaw to tighten and his eyes to narrow in anger that seemed to shift the energy around their bodies.

"Master Anzel?" another man called out.

"Take him to the magistrate."

Galon's heart pounded in terror, and his head and stomach danced in sick apprehension.

"I will bring the young midman along."

He closed his eyes, knowing well that he'd face a judgment of his own under Mages' law once the farmer was dealt with. This was a momentary reprieve, not a pardon of his crimes. No doubt the master was about to make that all too clear to him.

But did he see it? Or is he guessing? Not that it made a difference. If the master was of a mind to punish him, lack of first-hand knowledge of the facts wouldn't stay his hand.

Master Anzel dragged him to his feet, and Galon half-expected a good shaking to follow, but it didn't. Surprisingly, the master steadied Galon when he stumbled, standing straight and sure despite the burden of half-supporting another man's weight, staring down at Galon as if searching for something.

"Are you even old enough to travel alone, Midman?" he demanded.

Galon's face darkened. "Yes, Master. I reached twenty a season ago." He wouldn't offer the information that he'd been roaming for more than three seasons longer than that, though he'd answer the question truthfully if it was the next one asked.

"What is your name?"

"Galon of Outsten, Master." It wasn't strictly true. Since he'd been disowned by his family, he could claim no family affiliation, but that fact would raise more questions than he cared to answer this night.

He nodded, turning Galon toward the street. "Be mindful that you tell the magistrate the same lies you told myself and my guard, Midman Galon. You would be wise to."

A sob nearly knotted his throat. Galon swallowed it down painfully, unwilling to vent such a shameful emotion before his judge, certain now that Master Anzel had seen much more than Galon had hoped he had. "Yes, Master. As you say."

* * * *

It was all Anzel could do to keep a cork on his fury. Would there not have been too many questions about it, he would have ordered Talden to break the farmer's neck for daring so much.

He'd known this town was a dangerous one, and a midman hurrying into a darkened and deserted alleyway had raised the hair on Anzel's neck as nothing in years had.

They would have taken the farmer the moment his knife disappeared into his sheath had it not been for the look of pleasure on the young mage's face at his handling. Had it not gone badly from there, he would have left the young fool to his folly, but he'd admittedly tarried to see more of Galon's unabashed enjoyment reflected in his expressions.

Even now, that look affected Anzel, his cock reacting to the beautiful young face in the throes of passion.

Anzel allowed his gaze to settle on Galon's battered face for a moment, then forced his eyes away, feigning only a master's duty to protect a charge. His reason for looking away went deeper than what the night sleepers might make of his interest. Neither the tightening of his cock nor his heart was of use to him while this legal mess lay unsettled, and so he fought to control both.

"Master Anzel?" the magistrate asked. "What brings you here?"

Though they'd drawn the magistrate from his bed, a case involving a ravaged mage, brought to magistrate by a House An mage, brought swift results in the form of the magistrate dressing and joining them to do the honors in nearly record time.

He shot a look at the farmer, not bothering to hide his disgust with the foul creature. "This man stole from Midman Galon at knifepoint and then battered him."

"Nay!" the farmer protested. "It was sex play. The midman likes his partners rough. The money... I admit I was paid for my part, but if my tastes are not adverse and the coin will buy healing for my crops later in the season..." He shrugged with a dangerous smile.

Galon reeled on his feet, paling.

Anzel grasped him by the shoulder, steadying the youth, the cork coming unglued that quickly. He'd set out to teach the farmer a lesson. Now it was personal. He would see him punished to the full extent of the law, even if he had to lie to achieve it, as the farmer had just lied. No one questioned a House An mage, and the farmer would soon learn that.

"I saw no such thing," Anzel snapped. "Such a tired excuse, farmer. Can you find no better lie to tell? How many years has that one—"

"If there was no agreement, why did your midman follow me into the alleyway?"

He wasted not a moment, accepting the challenge. "Galon wasn't following you. He was attempting to find his way to my campsite to bargain for teaching. Talden had gone to find him when he was late. Thank the Mother for that!" He affected relief that wasn't far from the truth, considering his relief that they'd happened along when they did.

Galon glanced at Anzel out of the corner of his eye, then lowered his head, taking a calming breath. His entire body trembled beneath the steadying hand Anzel kept on his shoulder.

The magistrate broke the moment. "Is this true, Midman Galon?"

"Every word Master Anzel spoke, sir," he lied. "I lost my bearings. It was the ale, I suspect."

The farmer lunged at Galon, and Talden brought him up short. To Anzel's surprise, the midman didn't shy from the attack. He'd wondered at the young man's strength when he'd refused the farmer's order to beg for the sex he wanted. Now he had proof that Galon wasn't as weak as he'd appeared when he was attacked.

"Liar!" the farmer shouted. "You know the truth, boy."

"I do," Galon admitted, playing along with the game, "but you have proven that you do not. Or...you *care* not, whatever the case may be."

"Farmer Zelter," the magistrate barked. "The King's laws will be upheld. By witnesses three, you are judged guilty on both counts brought and on the charge of lying to a King's magistrate."

"Nay!" he protested again.

"The king's soldiers will take him from here, Guard Talden."

Anzel jerked his head to one side, looking at Zelter's waist meaningfully. Talden nodded, pulling Galon's pouch from the farmer's pocket and joining them.

"If you have no further need of us," Anzel hinted. He certainly had no use for the scowling farmer.

The magistrate bowed his head. "The moon is falling from its zenith and your night growing short. You should be on your way. Good journey, Master Anzel."

"May the Mother grant you easy dreams," he replied simply, then turned on his heel and led the way out, Galon and Talden at his back.

Galon whispered his thanks at the street, mayhap hoping that Anzel's lies marked his complicity in hiding the truth of Galon's life from all. A stern look from Anzel, coupled with a restraining hand on his shoulder from Talden, was all it took to still his feet.

"I will present myself at next moonrise," the midman vowed. His eyes were weary, and his gaze didn't tarry on Anzel's face. His shoulders slumped, and he seemed to draw in on himself even more markedly than moments before.

"You will accompany me now. Tell Talden where your camp is. He will collect your things and join us."

Galon hesitated, looking from one man to the other, then nodded. "Just off the side of the King's Road, east of town."

Talden turned without a word, and Anzel did the same. Galon fell into step behind him. A glance back showed the midman's arms crossed over his chest, his head bowed. Mother, but the boy was terrified of him.

As well he should be! It was a dangerous game Galon played...one that could see him dead someday, that almost saw him dead that very night.

At his camp, Anzel waved Galon into the tent. The midman crossed to the far corner and sank into it, seemingly making himself as small as possible. It spoke of years of misuse.

Anzel brought him a bowl of water from the bucket Talden kept full, grasping a clean rag on his way past the wash stand. Galon stared at them for a long moment and then took them with a muttered word of thanks.

He washed the blood from his face with tremulous hands, revealing the smooth skin and full lips beneath. His sad eyes remained hidden, trained on the dirt before his worn boots as if he'd learned in a long, painful manner that meeting the gaze of someone in power was to be avoided at all costs.

"Recite the three rules of travel, Midman Galon," he ordered, hoping to force the young man's face up.

It didn't work as he'd hoped it would. Galon stared into the bowl of bloodied water, answering in a strong but low and respectful voice. "Travel always with a thought to time and weather; be prepared as you may for both."

"We shall see," Anzel interjected, making it known that he would be inspecting all aspects of Galon's gear.

He nodded solemnly. "Pay always for your keep in coin or service; a Star Mage asks no charity. I do," he stated proudly, before Anzel could question it.

"Go on."

Galon grimaced. "Be always aware of your physical safety; put not yourself in danger, save for a noble cause." He waited for Anzel's condemnation.

"Would you care to list the *many* ways you have faulted on that third this night, or would you like me to name them for you?" he challenged.

Taking him literally, Galon began to speak. "I let myself be attacked in my inattention to my surroundings. I trusted... Nay, I knew the danger and chose to follow a potentially dangerous man away from the safety of light and numbers." He peeked up as if hoping he'd said enough to satisfy Anzel's anger.

Anzel arched a brow in answer.

Galon straightened and continued. "I let my base needs rule my sense of self-preservation," he mimicked, as if he'd been lectured thus before.

I should have shaken sense into him when first I reached him. "You do not even travel with a companion. Why is that?"

Midman Galon looked up, his expression aging his appearance by decades and his face darkening slightly. He didn't answer, but Anzel worked his way to it just the same.

"It is not that you cannot afford the keep of a companion. You cannot afford to pay him for his silence, for his discretion on the subject of your sexual leanings."

Galon looked away, his throat working hard, as if he held back some strong emotion...or fought a rising gorge.

Anzel sighed. That was one of the many things he had been blessed with that the midman had not. Anzel had money enough to buy the silence of his companions and power enough to silence them in other ways, if they dared cross him. None had from the day he had been invited to leave his grandfather's estate to this very day, and he doubted any would. One did not cross House An, even if they only protected Anzel to protect their precious name.

At his silence, Galon lowered his chin to his chest, hunching his shoulders as if preparing to protect his face and ribs from blows. A twinge of longing and compassion mixed lit in Anzel. Had he not been born into House An, he might be like this man: desperate, miserable, afraid, and friendless.

"Master Anzel?" Talden called from outside the tent.

"Set up Midman Galon's tent for yourself, Talden. Deliver his pallet and belongings to mine."

Galon looked up, fear and confusion warring in his dark eyes.

"We have much to discuss at the next moonrise, Midman Galon. For now, the moon is setting, and it has been too long a night for us all."

* * * *

Mey 13th, 3055

Galon laid on his bedroll, keeping very still in an effort not to disturb Master Anzel. He'd learned long ago not to invite attention, that one with the power to harm him most likely *would* harm him.

Still, he didn't understand the Master Mage.

He'd expected to take lashes, at least five for his disregard for the third rule of travel and another five or ten for being Mother cursed as desiring only male company on the sheets. Master Anzel had ordered none.

Yet, his mind taunted him.

Galon had expected the master to take the money his companion had liberated from Farmer Zelter, at least a portion of it in payment for the lies he'd told the magistrate to ensure Zelter's punishment. The pouch had been returned to him as heavy as it had left him...or nearly so. He hadn't dared count it.

For now. Only the Mother knows what Master Anzel may demand on the morrow.

Master Anzel had even provided washing water and an ointment to treat his injuries.

Will he do the same after the lashes?

That was unlikely. The best Galon could hope for was that the master meant to question him further, to feel out how many lashes he'd earned with his sexual drives.

A dim light invaded the light-blocking tent, a testament to the power of the sun that day. Usually, the misty sunlight wouldn't challenge such a fine cloth, but in a rare show of might, Galon could see nearly as well as he could on a half-moon night.

He'd seen such a sun before. He'd felt its burn. Tears misted his eyes, and Galon blinked them away, lying to himself that he simply needed to clear his fogged eyesight after that encounter from his memory. He unfisted his hands, forcing his eyes to focus on something...anything.

Having enough light to see wasn't a good thing. Seeing meant drinking in every line of Master Anzel's face.

It was impossible to accurately guess his age. Like all mages, he appeared younger than his years when compared with night sleepers. Only the touch of gray at his temples attested that he was more than five years Galon's senior, marking him at more than double that variance.

Anzel's face had just a touch of fat, lending soft curves to a landscape that included a strong jaw, almost too masculine to look fitting on the effeminate-featured mages, and a stark nose. His lips were dark and lush, his eyelashes long and thick, and his eyebrows full, lending a brooding quality to him in his slumber. Dark ringlets of hair surrounded his face and cascaded over his shoulders.

Mother, but his body was beautiful. Like his jaw, Master Anzel's shoulders were broad for a mage, his chest more finely etched than one of their kind normally was.

Moreover, he was powerful...in magic and in bodily form. Hefting Galon from the ground hadn't pressed the master, and when Galon had faltered in his balance, Master Anzel's hands and chest had given the impression of warm and welcoming walls. Just the memory of it made him shiver in delight.

"Galon?"

He startled, looking to Master Anzel in sick horror that he'd been caught staring at his host. If his erection was any indication, his wandering mind and sexual hunger had likely been all too apparent in his expression.

Two more lashes for that lapse in judgment? he taunted himself. Galon closed his eyes and curled into a ball on his bedroll, waiting for swift punishment that didn't come.

"Sleep, Galon," Master Anzel grumbled. "We have much to talk about when we wake."

"As you wish, Master." *Mayhap he is too tired to punish me now.* For that matter, Galon was too tired to take the lashes in a stoic manner.

He swallowed a sob at that. If there was one thing he'd learned, it was never to let them see you cry, and if he had to face lashes without sleep, he would surely cry.

* * * *

Anzel fisted his hand, forcing himself not to trace the cut on Galon's beautiful lips. He wanted to kiss the swollen break, to strip off the clothes the foolish boy had worn to bed, reveal his lean body, and experience the many delights of it.

When he'd woken and seen the stark hunger in Galon's eyes, it had been all Anzel could do not to drag the midman onto his pallet and see them both sated.

Mother, but that was madness! For one thing, he had no clue why Midman Galon affected him so. He was fourteen years Anzel's junior and seemingly set on his own destruction. Neither was something Anzel typically found appealing in a lover.

More notable, it was high day, and the night sleepers were moving about. With Talden asleep in Galon's tent, there was no guarantee that their passion wouldn't be overheard, and so Anzel forced himself to wait for moonrise, for a Star Mage's time to act.

Still his body was tight in need as he hadn't felt it since he was a man no older than Galon was now.

There was something about Galon... It wasn't simply his hunger; Anzel had met sexually-hungry men before. There was something broken in Galon, something shattered that Anzel felt certain he was meant to fix. Nay! He wanted to fix it. He needed to.

Galon's body relaxed as a body only does in sleep. He looked much younger that way, much more vulnerable.

"Sleep, Galon."

The soothing tone in his voice shook Anzel. Yet it felt right to him, and he murmured longer, senseless assurances that his young charge had nothing to fear. Then sleep took him.

* * * *

Galon was already awake when Anzel opened his eyes. To his favor, the midman hadn't left the tent. He was cleaning himself in near-silence with the same rag he'd used to wash his face the night before. The water he was wringing from it seemed to be clean, fresh water from the bucket, the foul no doubt disposed of in the waste bucket.

He stood at the wash stand, seemingly lost in his own thoughts. Oblivious as he was, the young mage didn't realize he had an audience as he drew his tunic off over his head to clean the travel dust from his skin.

Anzel's stomach knotted and churned in horror, threatening to empty of the sour acid that alone filled it. Galon had taken lashes, so many that separating one mark from another was a difficulty.

"How many times have you been judged on Mages' law?" he demanded, anger driving him. How dare Galon show such disregard for his life and self! Did he wish to die?

Galon turned, flipping the bowl to the floor in his haste. His eyes were wide and wild, and his chest and upper arms—

Anzel felt his face pale. His head spun, and he felt certain he would faint for the first time in his life.

The midman lowered his face in that damned abused slouch, trying to cover as much of his scarred chest as he could at once.

It wasn't a whip that had caused these scars. He'd been burned badly, what had surely resulted in blisters and fevering open sores a hundred times worse than his sealing scars.

"Once," Galon choked out. "Only once. I swear it, Master."

Anzel took to his feet, storming to Galon, noting his retreat to the tent wall in annoyance. He grasped the young man by one arm and turned him, forcing his hands to the edges of the wash station to bare the damage done to him.

Galon stiffened, his throat bobbing as if in need to cry out...or to cry. Realization that he was bracing himself for lashes came slowly.

Anzel didn't correct him. *Not yet. If he has lied to me, I may give him a new lash for it.* Somehow, Anzel doubted that he could bear to give Galon more than that, no matter how grievously he'd lied.

He touched the furrowed skin, and Galon shuddered. The midman's hands tightened on the wash station, and he ground his teeth audibly.

"Once?" Anzel challenged.

"Ten lashes, taken a little more than a year ago. The rest are old." Galon's voice was emotionless. A glance at his eyes showed them glazed, disconnected from the pain he believed he would feel.

"For what reason?" he asked more gently, certain now that Galon was telling him the truth.

He was inexplicably touched by the young midman's stoic response.

"You know what I am. What I prefer on the sheets." It was a cold fact to him, stated without embellishment.

"Your family did this? The rest of the damage?"

Galon nodded.

"But...why? King's law has no— Or...was your father a Star Mage?" That made no sense, even as Anzel said it. Galon claimed it had nothing to do with Mages' law, and Anzel believed him.

The midman's bark of laughter unnerved him. It was a half-mad sound, accompanied by a manic grin.

"No. He was a simple farmer who was blessed enough to produce a mage." The laugh that followed was no less frightening. "They wanted an heir from me, another young mage to exploit for their own gain when they cast me out."

"And?" Anzel prompted him, bracing himself mentally for something worse.

"He paid a woman to bear for me, but..." His smile faded, replaced with the look of detachment that announced how the memories hurt him as nothing else would have. "I prefer men on my sheets," he whispered.

"You could not perform with a woman?" he guessed. It wasn't unheard of. Anzel wasn't able to complete with a woman himself.

"The only way I could..." He shook his head, his throat bobbing again.

"A massage?" he offered as delicately as he could.

"Yes. It was the only way I stayed erect long enough."

"And the burns?" Some sane corner of his mind argued that Anzel didn't want the answer to that question, but he asked it anyway.

"Sun exposure. They protected what they considered the essential—" Galon paused for a moment. "I fathered a girl instead of the boy they wanted."

Anzel's knees buckled, and he landed on his arse on Galon's bedroll.

Blind to the world around him, the midman kept talking. "Orana was one year last season. I imagine they hope she will produce a young mage when she comes of age for it. Nay, I know that is their wish. I can only hope they don't hire out for a stud for—"

"You allow that? You accept it?" he asked dumbly.

"I wasn't given a choice in the matter." His breathing hitched, then returned to a smooth flow, no doubt by force of will alone.

"She is your child. You have rights to her. How could you leave her to them?" Anzel demanded, heartsick at the idea of it.

There was a moment of silence. "What have I to offer her? No home. Uncertain meals and shelter." Despite his most valiant effort, Galon's voice went rough in emotion.

"Sit with me, Galon. We have much to discuss." Much more than he'd anticipated, by far.

* * * *

Galon forced his breathing to even and his white-knuckled hands to unclench, numbly concluding that Anzel wasn't about to lay lashes on him.

Yet.

He turned from the wash station on trembling legs and half-sank/half-fell to his bedroll.

"You play a dangerous game," Anzel whispered.

"I have needs, as any man does." Galon had ceased apologizing for that when Master Eldor had betrayed him. "I cannot be what I am not. I sate my drives as I must, in the only way I can."

"And when you were caught and—"

"I was not caught. I have never been *caught.*" His heart ached at the truth of that.

"I do not understand."

"My father sent me to...a master after what he calls my 'failure to produce a son.' He knew the ways to touch, ways one does not know unless he has played in a man's body before."

"Go on," Master Anzel urged him.

"I believed he was Mother-sent to me, that I was not alone in my inclinations." Galon paused again, pierced through the heart by the memories. "I found him abed with a local woman. It seemed he was of a type that beds indiscriminately. That day, he hungered for a female hole.

"I was lost. I would have taken any scrap of kindness from him. I begged him for his love, for his body...for whatever he would grant me."

Anzel winced. "Is that why you refused to beg Farmer Zelter, though it might have meant your death?"

He nodded resolutely. It was one vow he'd never broken. Even his vow not to cry before one who could hurt him had been tossed aside when he was exposed to the harsh rays of the sun that seared his sensitive mage's skin. He shook his head, knocking loose the memories of his screams, his pleas for release.

Anzel's voice drew Galon out of his phantom pains. "He cast you aside?"

"He had me whipped. He laughed with the whore who shared his bed. I ran...as soon as I was able to walk."

The master fell into a deep silence that made Galon's nerves jump. Mayhap he'd said too much, but talking to Master Anzel was strangely easy.

"And you will take men again." The master didn't question it.

Neither did Galon deny it. "I sate my needs as I must and can."

"You would indulge with me, if I were willing." Again, he didn't question that he spoke the truth.

As if he should? Surely, Galon's lust had been impossible to miss when he'd been caught staring at high day.

Farmer Zelter was right. I am a whore, spreading for nearly any man who intrigues me. And Anzel was the kind of man who intrigued him, at least as far as his strength, his power, his command of those around him.

"Would you, Galon?"

"Yes," he breathed. "Mother curse me, I would."

Anzel leaned toward him, wrapping one hand around the back of his neck. It took only a moment for Galon to piece together that the master wasn't planning him immediate harm as Zelter had. Though the lips crushed to his aggravated the split in his lip, the master's hungry moan was proof enough that Anzel didn't *mean* to cause him pain.

Galon parted his lips, meeting the master in a true lover's kiss. At the enthusiastic response, he chanced laying his hands on Anzel's chest. The increased vigor of their joining urged Galon on.

He unbuttoned the master's trousers, freeing the cock within, one that was undeniably as ready as his own. Trembling in restraint, Galon took Anzel's measure, handling him into the release of early fluids.

Anzel's mouth left his, returning to stroke gently over the swelling on his lip. "You call this a curse?"

"Not this." *What comes later, though...* Galon pushed away that thought as a concern for later. For now, he wanted to believe...to feel...and nothing more than that.

Master Anzel aided in that by returning the favor of unbuttoning Galon's trousers. His hunger transformed his face into a fierce mask that said sex would be incendiary. "Once here." He breathed his cryptic comment into Galon's chest.

"And then?" Galon dared to ask. Would it be another Master Eldor? Lashes and unkind words once the master had his climax, though it was clear that Anzel shared at least a smattering of his taste for male flesh?

A thought for later.

Unless he speaks it true now. Then what will I do?

At least I will know where I stand. Lashes have been expected since the moment he stood over me, and Farmer Zelter would have done worse.

"We will travel to my home. On horseback...and using back trails, we can reach it before moonset, if we press."

Galon's question of why the master would demand such a thing was lost in another searing kiss. The future was suddenly unimportant. He'd lived from moment to moment for a year, and this moment was one worth living, no matter what came next.

The rest was a blur of discovery, hands and mouths testing and teasing, clothing being cast away to the corners of the tent. A mage's magic sizzled along their skin as they touched, taunting Galon with memories of mage on mage sex. It was something he'd thought he'd never experience again.

In moments, they were spooned together, Anzel pressed to Galon's back, his fingers testing the stretch of the passage, lubricating it with the fluids Galon had raised. The moment of consummation passed smoothly and without question, as if they'd been lovers for years instead of that very hour.

Galon half-stifled a moan at the retreat of Anzel's fingers. The crown of the master's cock spread him, working past the ring of muscle in a delicious little shimmy. Anzel's abdominal muscles tightened against Galon's lower back, and the master's hips shifted, forcing his cock further.

"Yes." The plea was out before Galon could censor himself.

Anzel thrust deeper. His hand settled on Galon's shoulder, pulling him closer and pushing him down onto the pillar of that glorious cock in a single motion.

Galon wriggled further, seeking all the master had to give. As if in answer, Anzel's hips jerked up, and his cock pulsed against the walls of Galon's ass.

It was too much. Galon gave in and moaned in pleasure. As if that was the master's breaking point, he started thrusting hard, gasps and shudders escaping him.

Anzel outlasted him but only by moments. In the aftermath, they lay together, Anzel's arms holding Galon close at the shoulders, their breathing harsh in his ears, their cocks slowly lessening.

The master moved, leaving Galon's body and rolling him to his back. He met Anzel's gaze steadily, the thud of his heart marking the time until bliss would turn to agony in body and soul.

Anzel lowered his head, laying a lick on the cum-coated head of Galon's cock, a gift that few had ever granted Galon in his life. The sensation was too much, and he hardened again, biting back a scream of pleasure.

"At my home, you need not hide your sounds," Anzel offered. Galon forced his jaw to unclench, going boneless in relaxation.

Anzel was suddenly towering over him, pulling a fresh pair of trousers from his pack. "Dress, Galon. The moon is rising, and I intend to have you on my sheets at next moonrise." He paused, a devastating smile lighting his face.

Galon's heart stuttered at that.

"And perhaps in my tub shortly after that."

At Galon's hesitation, Anzel stared at him. The master knelt at his side and laid a soft kiss on his mouth.

"Come." The kiss might have been soft, but his voice was rough, though Galon suspected it was rough in arousal and not in an edge of violence.

He nodded, reaching for his pack, and Anzel's smile widened. Galon had no idea why, but he knew without question that he would travel the circumference of Terra Set to see Anzel smile.

* * * *

Mey 21st, 3055

"I have only one test left of you to prove that you are a mason," Anzel informed him.

Galon nodded, holding himself rigid in a sure sign that he was frightened half to death by the concept that he was about to be elevated.

It was something he'd never dared consider pursuing for himself, Anzel knew. Seeking out a master to train him to elevate would bring attention down on him and risk exposing his inclinations to one with the power to punish him for it.

Worse, if the master was acquainted with Master Eldor, who knew what punishment might lay in store for him.

"Remove your tunic, Midman Galon."

He hesitated, looking around at the deserted field as if fearing an audience.

"They are my fields. No one would dare. Remove your tunic."

Galon ducked his chin toward his chest, pulling off the fine cotton tunic and folding it over the fence beside him. He started to cover his chest, then lowered his arms, peeking up at Anzel as if afraid he'd be counseled again for trying to hide himself from his master and lover.

"Better. To elevate to mason, you must be schooled in the art of how touch increases the output of a shared channeling."

"I cannot." The pain in his voice was heartbreaking.

"You can," Anzel assured him. He pulled off his own tunic and tossed it negligently over Galon's, striding toward him.

"I cannot," he insisted. "You know how I would react. Though any mage would be likely to harden under the circumstances, I am too expressive to touch and want and hide it from others."

The moon was strong, strong enough to make the power surge in Anzel's body, bringing him half-erect in the rush of energy alone. It would take very little of Galon's body to do the rest.

"Touch me," he invited. "You can touch me." Anzel dipped his head, pressing his lips to Galon's throat just above the scars that maimed him.

"Are you mad?" he whispered, his breathing going ragged.

"Touch me, Galon. Feed me your power and earn your brown mason's robes."

His hand pressed flat to Anzel's chest, stroking down the line of his ribs to the soft expanse of his belly. "You are mad." But it was said without censure...and without conviction.

"Mad for you," he countered. He was. The combination of Galon's body and the power rising between them had Anzel hard and aching. He pressed at Galon's arse, bringing the erect length behind his trousers into close contact with the one behind Galon's.

Galon moaned, then bit his lip to hold back his sounds.

"Don't. We will touch. We will share our bodies—"

"Here?" He gasped.

Convincing him wouldn't be difficult; Galon lost all sense of propriety when properly motivated. "Yes. Now, must I order you to touch me, or will you do so willingly?"

"I still say you are mad." His stroking hands made it clear that Galon no longer cared how mad it was.

The power between them spiked along with their arousal. It was always thus, the interconnected sensations of channeling and sexual need. One would always spur the other.

At the edges of control, Anzel drew Galon's mouth up for a kiss not unlike their first.

The young mage had a mouth that would prompt Anzel to beg for more, if Galon asked for such a thing. The first time Galon took his length into his mouth, Anzel had felt faint in pleasure. The second had been even better; they had taken each other in unison that night, then slept in each other's arms.

Galon didn't ask what he wanted. It amazed Anzel how quickly his lover had learned his tastes and started anticipating his mind.

The midman's hand worked at freeing Anzel's cock, and he left the kiss, trailing his mouth down Anzel's body with a groan of pleasure. Anzel used the fence for support, his knees going weak at the promise of the liquid heat of Galon's sweet mouth.

Then he was there, his tongue circling the head in teasing, his fingers stroking the sheath covering it back to bare the most sensitive tip to his wicked attentions. It was all Anzel could do to stay on his feet, floored nearly as much by Galon's power as he was by the mage's sexual prowess.

The power was drugging, and his skin burned in the very visible sparks of their consummation at the sharing. Anzel moaned at the idea of soulbinding with Galon. How much power would they generate in that joining? In that moment of passion and commitment to their union?

"Do not tease, Galon," he pleaded, giving up the pretense of order. "Take me in. Mother, I cannot last much longer."

Neither the rising power between them nor the rising arousal would allow that. Though Anzel could well channel the power slowly into the crops around them, he had something special planned, something that would take a great deal of power, and so he wasn't willing to squander it.

Galon pulled him in deep, stroking with a purpose to making Anzel spend in long, hard spasms that would leave him weak as a babe. And he succeeded admirably, drinking down Anzel's seed like a man stumbling from a desert would drink down water.

Anzel fisted his hand in Galon's hair, forcing his working mind to focus on his goal. He released the power in a rush, with almost as little conscious control as he had over his escaping seed.

The weeds that had overtaken the fence line in his absence transformed into a line of azca berry bushes, then matured and bore fruit in a matter of moments. The scents of new leaves, pungent flowers, and sweet fruit teased at his already overloaded senses.

Galon released him, turning to the bushes with wild eyes. Anzel caught at his shoulder, using the grip to ease himself to his knees beside his lover.

"I do not understand," Galon admitted.

Anzel shook his head, searching for the words to express it. "With the right partner, touch can work wonders, Galon."

"Yes, but—"

"You told me that you favor azca berries. Consider them a gift on your elevation to mason."

Anzel couldn't be certain whether Galon's shock was caused by the fact that he'd been elevated or by the fact that Anzel had given him a gift so personal. Either way, his silence made Anzel nervous. "There is one condition."

Galon looked to him, guarded. "Which would be what?"

"Ripe azca berries are known to drip juice down the body of he who eats them. The juice that drips is mine to taste, my love."

His lover's agreement came in the form of grasping a berry and crushing it to his chest.

* * * *

Juno 15th, 3055

"It is madness— You are mad!"

Anzel smiled, then wider as Galon hardened. Mother, all it took was a smile to make him respond.

"It is not madness. It is right," he explained patiently. "All your reasons are no more. My home is yours...unless you mean to leave me."

His heart ached that Galon might choose to do it. It would be the ultimate horror, to have his lover leave him when he'd finally found one he would soulbind with, if Galon proved willing.

Galon paled, shaking his head in a seeming horror that matched Anzel's. That was a good sign, though it had taken more than a week after reaching his home to convince Galon they had no need to hide their relationship.

"N—never," the young mason stammered out. "You know I..." He swallowed hard, dropping his gaze in a sign of his uncertainty.

Anzel urged his chin up, reminding his lover that it annoyed him silently. "Say it when you are ready."

In the three weeks since their shared channeling in his fields, Galon had stopped himself short of professing his love at every turn. Anzel knew it bothered Galon that Anzel could profess his feelings openly, and his young lover could not, but years of mistrust were not easily overcome.

Anzel had no doubts that Galon loved him. It showed in every tender kiss and touch, every kind look and blush. The words would come when they did.

Galon nodded, his throat bobbing and his face darkening, as if he longed to let the words burst free.

"Along the while, though..." Anzel caressed Galon's lips with his thumb, stroking the white line of knitting tissue, the only sign left of the farmer's brutal attack. "Know that I do love you."

"It is still madness." His voice was strong and sure on that point.

"Why? Have my servants shown disrespect for you? For us? Have the townspeople? The shopkeeps who measured you for your new robes and clothes?"

Galon shook his head slowly, his eyes wary. Anzel had seen this defensive posture before. Like his inability to express the words of love, it was something that would take time to overcome.

But Galon was a Star Mage. The power was his, and he would learn to grasp it in time.

Anzel continued, needing to drive home the point that eluded Galon at every turn of the world. "King's law supports what we are, Galon. You know that."

"What of Mages' law?" he asked nervously. "Would you risk it to love me openly? Why would you do such a thing?"

"They only dared touch you when you were of no family. Estranged from my house or not, you now have the protection of House An, because you are my love."

"But—"

"Mage's law only says we must reproduce if we are able. We have a daughter, Galon...if you would allow me to claim Orana as such. We have only to collect her."

He took a calming breath, no doubt trying to reason a more effective argument.

It was time to shake Galon's world view a bit. The next logical argument he'd make would likely be that House An would never accept Orana as Anzel's child. "Of course, once Orana is with us, we could try for a younger brother or sister for her," he half-teased, his heart hammering at Galon's possible response to that.

Galon's eyes narrowed. "How do you intend to do that?" He leaned back, distancing himself on the bed.

Anzel forced himself not to wince. For Galon, either possibility would seem torture. His father's brutal quest for an heir would make the idea of Galon taking a woman unpalatable. After Master Eldor's betrayal, the thought of Anzel taking a woman, as impossible as it was, would wound him even more.

He smiled, stroking his fingertips over Galon's still-hard cock. "Be honest, my love. When I mount you, you lose yourself."

His expression was abruptly hungry. "You know I do."

"I know women who would share a bed with us and carry our children."

Galon blanched. "Whose children, Anzel?"

"Ours. It is true that I cannot complete in a woman, but with you to suckle me to climax and a woman's body there to catch the seed—"

"And?" He was a perceptive man. It served him well, as always.

"Would it be so terrible for me to love you, to arouse you so that she could take you in? She would be only a vessel to catch your seed, Galon." He hurried on, hoping to put Galon at ease with the idea...to at least cause him to consider the possibility. "With both of us depositing to her, no one could say for certain whose child slept in the womb. It would be both of ours, undeniably."

Galon didn't reply, leaving Anzel to wonder at his silence. Mayhap he'd pushed too hard and too fast.

"If you cannot face it, we will spoil Orana alone," Anzel conceded. "She will be the child of my heart. You have my vow on that."

"The mages would have to admit we were doing our duty to reproduce," Galon whispered, lost in thought.

Anzel's heart skipped a beat in excitement. "Indeed, they would."

"And House An would have to acknowledge the children as your own or risk embarrassment."

"They would." His grandfather and father would not be pleased, but they'd never been pleased where Anzel was concerned.

"I suppose any sons born of the union would have to be given House An names."

"To force them to acknowledge them as my heirs, they would...but you could choose the names," he offered.

Galon met Anzel's gaze. "I will consider it. I can offer no more than that."

"It is blessing enough."

His young lover chuckled, a sound Anzel thought he might never hear. "You might have to convince me," he warned.

"You know I enjoy the challenge of it."

* * * *

Juno 20th, 3055

Galon slid from his saddle, taking a calming breath. Anzel stepped to his side, offering comfort and strength silently. Talden stood at his opposite shoulder, ordered there by Anzel for Galon's protection. Finally, two House An royal bodyguards took their places at their backs. Galon was grateful for them, though he knew they were cousins of Anzel's, only there because Anzel called them in and traded this service in settlement of some debt they owed him.

The cool night wind whipped Galon's brown mason's robes and pressed the silk tunic beneath to his scarred flesh. He'd come in his finest, hoping it would make a believer of himself more than his father.

As if reading his thoughts, Anzel spoke. "You are not the boy who ran any longer."

255

The choice not to touch Galon in comfort had been mutually agreed upon. If his parents saw such a move and guessed their relationship, it would be all the harder to free Orana. This way, they were master and student, and his father need know no more than that.

Galon nodded and strode to the door, his guards and Anzel taking his lead.

The door opened as he reached it. His mother looked from face to face, seemingly struck mute by the group of individuals she faced. Galon noted that she couldn't meet his gaze in grim satisfaction.

A memory shattered the calm of his mind, and Galon forced himself to weather it, showing not a thimbleful of the pain it caused him.

"Orana. We have to name her Orana, Ragel. I always wanted a daughter named Orana."

"And all the Mother granted was a daughter named Galon."

"Selana of Outsten," he greeted her coldly, hating her for never once arguing his father's cruelty.

She flinched.

"You have something that belongs to me. I have come to collect the debt."

The gruff voice from the darkened room made his blood run cold. "You own nothing here. I paid with sweat and coin for everything within."

Selana was pushed aside, and Ragel took her place in the doorway.

His father met Galon's eyes solidly. The smell of stale ale and sweat was heavy on him.

After a moment, Galon pulled the pouch from his belt, heavy in his coin and Anzel's combined. "You paid twenty silver coin for Orana's birth and a year of nursing."

"Plus food for the nurse and keeping for the child," he snapped.

"Another thirty more than covers that."

"What of the loss of a year of your service? Do you plan to pay me that, as well?" His smile was calculating, without warmth or remorse for a son wronged.

"You were relieved of my keeping."

"You know the return on the crops would have outweighed that."

"Not a brass," he vowed.

"Then what is within remains my own." His arched brow and drunken swagger of another step toward Galon announced his perceived victory.

Galon snapped his fingers, and Ragel looked at him in confusion.

"Leesa," Anzel ordered. "Raeshel."

They slipped past Galon's shoulder, through the space Anzel had vacated. In a moment, the two royal bodyguards had his father immobilized, a dagger to his sagging throat, a sign of years of decadence in food and drink.

Selana stood in stunned silence.

Galon marched smartly through the house to the room that had once been his. He smiled at the sight of Orana, standing in the crib that had seen generations of Outstens, her tiny fists wrapped around the rail.

He lifted her, cuddling his daughter into the folds of his robes to shield her from the chill

257

outside. Then he turned his back on the house and people, shoving the fifty in the pouch at Selana on his way past. They would have what they paid for the child and no more.

"Not a brass," he repeated. Galon had paid more than enough in blood and scars, more than enough to buy Orana, but it was the one thing Ragel and Selana could argue before a magistrate, and so he gave them that small victory of him in the leaving.

Anzel was speaking to Ragel in a low, dangerous voice. Galon didn't pause to hear it. He knew the sentence being passed, since they'd discussed it at length. It was to be thirty lashes at Talden's hand, and Talden had a strong arm, easily a match for Ragel's.

It was a sentence that Ragel didn't dare complain to a magistrate about, though Anzel had no right to deal it out to a night sleeper. Doing so would mean that Galon would be invited to defend his lover to the magistrate, and in doing so, Ragel would face much worse for his crimes: more lashes and forced labor, most likely, though exposing Galon to sunlight as he had could carry a sentence of death. No, Ragel didn't dare take that route, as Galon hadn't for so long.

He'd convinced Anzel not to brand Ragel with hot pokers, but only by a narrow margin. Even now, Galon wasn't entirely sure his father would be spared that punishment once he and Raeshel had Orana out of earshot of it.

His daughter laughed in glee as he swung into the saddle, her hand touching his face.

Galon turned his mount, Raeshel at his side, warmth spreading through him. All that mattered was Orana, Anzel, and their new life together. He'd never ask Anzel if Ragel took brands. If he did, Ragel was due them, and it had nothing to do with Galon now.

* * * *

Juno 28th, 3055

Galon sighed, shutting the door to Orana's room quietly. Though she'd been there a week and had settled into her new home and true family with no difficulty, he still felt the need to check on her several times as she slept.

He paused in the doorway to the room he shared with Anzel, taking a moment to appreciate his lover's flawless skin and silken hair.

"She is breathing and not half-starved?" Anzel teased.

"As if you will not be a nervous father with our first together?" he countered.

More and more, Galon had been considering Anzel's plan. If it would protect them from Mages' law and allow Anzel the same sort of wonder he felt at a child of his own flesh, it was a small price to pay for it.

Anzel's eyes lit in excitement. "Should I call for a surrogate?" he offered.

Galon loosened the tie on his sleeping robe, dropping it to the floor. He slid into bed, feeling for the first time the noble Anzel proclaimed him at every opportunity. He had the power to make Anzel smile, and that was a great power, indeed.

"Galon? Do not tease me so."

"I am *almost* convinced."

A predatory look settled on his face. "You are a challenge."

"And you love a challenge, do you not, my love?" He loved *being* that challenge.

Anzel stared at him in amazement.

It was true, and it was long past time to say it. "I love you."

Anzel's smile made the world spin faster.

The End

About the Author

Brenna Lyons wears many hats, sometimes all on the same day: former president of EPIC, author of more than 100 published works, owner of Fireborn Publishing, columnist, special needs teacher, wife, mother...and member in good standing of more than 60 writing advocacy groups.

In her first ten years published in novel-length, she's won 3 EPIC e-Book Awards (out of 15 finalists) and finaled for 3 PEARLS (including one Honorable Mention, second to NY Times Bestseller Angela Knight), 2 CAPAS, and a Dream Realm Award. She's also taken Spinetingler's Book of the Year for 2007.

Brenna writes in 26 established worlds plus stand-alones, poetry, articles and essays. She's a bestseller in indie/e fantasy and horror, straight genre and cross-genres thereof. Brenna has been termed "one of the most deviant erotic minds in the publishing world...not for the weak." (Rachelle for Fallen Angels Reviews) Milieu-heavy dark work is practically Brenna's calling card, with or without the erotic content.

She teaches classes in everything from POV studies to advanced editing, networking to marketing. Brenna enjoys hearing from people who read her work and can be reached by e-mail.

Website: http://www.brennalyons.com/

Facebook:
http://www.facebook.com/brenna.lyons

Email: brennalyons4168@live.com

Also by this Author

Available from *Fireborn Publishing*

KEIF'S DEN AND PACK
Keif's Pack
Mother of the Keif
Keif's Den (Coming Soon)

PROPHECY
Prophecy: Revelations
Prophecy: Rapture
The Prophet's Mate
Prophecy: Rampage - Meet Gavin
Prophecy: Rampage (Coming Soon)

RENEGADES SERIES
TYGERS
Renegade's Run
Max Sec

THE FANTASY CLUB
The Consort

INSTINCT SERIES
Animal Instincts

KEGIN SERIES
Earth-Born Lord
Graham: Training the Earth-Born Lord

NIGHT WARRIORS
Claiming a Lady
Stone Lord
Mother's Son
Night Warriors

Will of the Stone
Bearing Armen
Hunter's Tales
Maher Men
The Blutjagdfrau Chronicles
Veriel's Tales I: Crossbearer Turned
Veriel's Tales II: Losing Regana

URBAN GRIMM
Catch Me, If You Can
Three Wishes
Temptation of Eve

WEREWOLF U
Werewolf U
Younger Daughter
Alpha Son
Never Alone
Her Christmas Wolves

ANGEL-WING SAGA
Sons of Heaven: Beldon
Sons of Heaven: Unexpected Mates
Daughters of Man: Prize Match
Daughters of Man: Claiming a Princess

COLOR OF LOVE
The Color of Love

KEGIN SERIES
Conquest
The Last of Fion's Daughters
Last Chance for Love
Rites of Mating
In Her Ladyship's Service
Matchmaker's Misery

KIELAN SERIES
The Lady's Lowborn Lover

Once in a Blue Moon
Overtime Pay
Stay With Me
The Fire God's Woman
Nevermore
Bride Ball
Undead in Blue
Mama's Tales
Unexpected Daddy
We Shall Live Again
May the Best Man Win
Marked
And It Was Good
Monsters of Myth Anthology

Available from **Under The Moon**

Evil Overlords Union Issue #1 Anthology
Undead Embrace
"*Playing Games*" in *Forbidden Love: Bad Boys*
"*Marked*" in *Forbidden Love: Wicked Women*
"*The Master's Lover*" in *Forbidden Love: Sacred Bands*

Available from **Logical Lust**

"*Mine for the Night*" in *The Cougar Book* Anthology

Available from **Coming Together Charity Anthologies**

INSTINCT SERIES
"*Foundling*" in *Coming Together: Into the Light* Anthology

"*Claim Mate*" (available separately and as part of the
Coming Together: Against the Odds Anthology)
"*The Fire God's Woman*" in *Coming Together: Under Fire*
Anthology

Available **self-published**

Snapshots from a Poet's Life

Award-Winning Books

EPPIE/EPIC eBOOK AWARDS WINNERS
Coming Together: Against the Odds- 2010
Time Currents- 2010
Coming Together: Into the Light- 2011

EPPIE/EPIC eBOOK AWARDS FINALISTS
Fion's Daughter- 2004
Collected Poems: Book One- 2005 (now titled *Snapshots of a Poet's Life*)
Renegade's Run- 2005
Rites of Mating- 2006
All I Want for Christmas- 2006
Phaze in Verse- 2008
"The Fire God's Woman" in Coming Together: Under Fire- 2009
Three Wishes- 2010
Matchmaker's Misery- 2010
The Cougar Book- 2011
The Master's Lover- 2011
Bride Ball- 2011

DREAM REALM AWARDS FINALIST
Last Chance for Love- 2003

PEARL HONORABLE MENTION
Night Warriors- 2004

PEARL FINALISTS
Schente Night- 2003 (now included in *The Last of Fion's Daughters*)
König Cursebreakers- 2004 (now titled *Will of the Stone*)

JOYFULLY REVIEWED BEST BOOKS OF 2010
Written in the Stars- 2010

SPINETINGLER'S BOOK OF THE YEAR 2007
NOBODY: An Anthology of Dark Fiction- 2007 (Brenna's
pieces of the anthology can be found in *Beyond the Veil*)

TRS's CAPA FINALISTS
Ultimate Warriors- 2004 (Brenna's portion is now
available as *With Great Power*)
Written in the Stars

LOVE ROMANCE AND MORE CAFÉ BOOK OF THE
YEAR RUNNER UP
Last Chance for Love- 2008

ROAD TO ROMANCE REVIEWERS' CHOICE
AWARD
Prophecy: Revelations- 2004

LOVE ROMANCES REVIEWERS' CHOICE AWARD
Black Sail- 2003

ROMANCE JUNKIES BOOK CLUB STAFF PICK
TYGERS- 2003

FALLEN ANGELS ROMANCE RECOMMENDED
READ
Devon's Price-2005 (now available in *Bearing Armen*)

JOYFULLY RECOMMENDED READ
Fairy Dreams- 2008
The Last of Fion's Daughters- 2009

TREBLE HEART FINALIST
Prophecy: Revelations- 2003

www.ingramcontent.com/pod-product-compliance
Lightning Source LLC
Chambersburg PA
CBHW050719180626
46814CB00002B/507